Chronicles of Eldoria: Eye of Shadows
Breezy Grooms

Dedication

For my great uncle, Steve—
You always believed in me, even when this dream was just a whisper in my heart.

This book is my promise fulfilled.
You once told me, "A good writer can make the characters seem human, but the best writer makes the characters come alive."
I have carried those words with me, and I hope I have done them justice.

I hope you're watching

"Fate does not bind the strong, but the strong do not escape its grasp."
—Aegyptean War Hymns

"To wield great power is to bargain with the abyss. The question is not what you gain—but what you lose."
—Elysian Scholar

"Wars are not won by kings or conquerors. They are won by the forgotten, the nameless, the dead."
—Stormrheim War Codex

"Light and shadow are not enemies, but reflections of the same truth."
—Teachings of the First Raevnir

Acknowledgments

This story was not written in solitude, but with the love and support of those who have stood beside me.

To my parents, Susan and Gary, who have shaped me with their unwavering belief, your encouragement has been my strength.

To my fiancé, Zhanae—Mir'shava, my heart, my anchor in the storm—thank you for your patience, your faith, and for always reminding me why I write. Your love is woven into every word, every page.

To my friends, who have listened to my ramblings, debated lore with me, and never let me give up—this book carries a piece of you all.
For every late-night idea, every word of encouragement, and every moment shared in this journey—thank you.
This book exists because of you.

PROLOGUE
The Fall of Rhexion

"Every beginning is the echo of a forgotten end."—Teachings of the First Raevnir

Legends are born in blood.

This one was no different.

Once, Eryndor stood as a beacon of power, its marble spires gleaming beneath the sun, its warriors feared across the continent. The halls of its great citadel echoed with the voices of scholars, rulers, and warriors alike, all bound by the unyielding will of their king.

The great kingdom of Eryndor burned.

Smoke choked the streets, thick enough to blot out the stars. Figures ran through the ruins—soldiers locked in final battles, children screaming for mothers who would never answer. The river ran black with soot, carrying ash instead of water.

Flames rose like twisted banners against the darkened sky, licking hungrily at shattered stone, at ruined towers, at bodies long since abandoned to the streets. The air was thick with ash and death, the scent of destruction woven into the very fabric of the land. Eyndor had become a tomb.

And at its center—

A king stood alone.

Rhexion was no fool.

He had known from the moment he took the crown of Eryndor that his reign would end not in peace, but in war.

But this—this was not war.

This was annihilation.

The throne room lay in ruin, its marble floors split open by fractures of molten rock. Rhexion stood before the broken remains of his kingdom, his once-proud armor stained with blood—some his, most not.

The throne of Eryndor—once carved from obsidian and gold—was now split down the middle, its jagged halves like broken fangs in the firelight. The banners of his ancestors hung in tatters, their sigils unrecognizable beneath the smoke.

Beyond the shattered hall, the beast loomed.

Rhexion had called for a dragon.

Instead, something else had answered.

It was a thing of shadow and ruin, its form shifting like a storm made flesh. Where its wings should have been, there was only the writhing of something ancient, something wrong. Its eyes—two burning voids—bored into him, and Rhexion felt his very soul tremble.

It had many names.

But tonight, it was simply his executioner.

"You sought power, little king."

Its voice was a blade, curling around him like an assassin's whisper.

"You sought the Eye."

The Eye of Shadows.

The artifact men would burn empires for.

The artifact Rhexion had spent his entire life hunting.

He had found it.

And it had found him.

"Was it worth it?" the creature murmured.

The question slithered through the burning throne room, wrapping around his throat like an unseen noose.

Rhexion did not answer.

Rhexion thought of the men who died believing in him. Of the promise he had made. The throne he had sworn to protect. The Eye had been his salvation—but all it had brought was ruin. Yet, even now, he would not kneel.

Instead, he raised his blade.

Even in ruin, he was still a king.

His hand trembled, not with fear—never fear—but with the weight of the choice he had made.

He had sought the Eye to protect his people.

He had sought it to end war, not bring it.

And yet—

Here he stood.

Alone.

The creature laughed.

It did not move, but the shadows around it pulsed, as though feeding off the despair of the world it was about to claim.

"Brave."

The word was almost… amused.

But amusement was not mercy.

Power surged.

The last king of Eryndor steeled himself.

And then—

The world turned to darkness.

The fall of Eryndor was written in history as a warning.

A kingdom lost. A king swallowed by shadow.

The Eye of Shadows—gone.

But legends are not just warnings.

They are promises.

And those who listen closely enough can still hear the whispers of a king who never died.

Waiting.

Watching.

And in the echoes of time, one truth remains—

The Eye was lost.

But the Eye will wake again. Some say Rhexion never died. That his soul was bound to the Eye, waiting for the day it would be found again. Others whispered that he still walks the ruins of Eryndor, neither man nor ghost—just a king who will never rest.

Chapter One

Shadows Over Mythralis

"No blade is sharper than belief."—Aegyptean War Hymns

☐

The smell of sea spray clung to Dorian's skin as he moved through the docks, weaving between sailors from the different continents unloading crates of silks, pottery, leather goods, perfumes, furs, and foreign spices. The sun hung low over the harbor, casting streaks of gold, pink, and violet across the water and wooden planks.

The marketplace was alive with noise—traders arguing, merchants haggling, stalls closing for the night, the occasional laugh from a drunk stumbling out of a tavern, mingling with the distant clatter of hooves on cobblestone. Dorian took it all in with sharp, calculating eyes, scanning the crowd for an opportunity.

The city had a rhythm, a pulse. You could feel it if you listened close enough—the rise and fall of trade, of whispered deals in the shadowed alleys, of sailors spending their coin faster than they earned it. The scent of roasted meat and fresh bread mingled with the stink of unwashed bodies, fish guts, and seaweed left rotting on the docks. A beggar rattled a tin cup near a spice vendor, ignored by everyone. A pickpocket, younger than Dorian, worked the crowd, slipping a purse from a distracted noble before vanishing into the side streets. Smart kid.

Dorian adjusted his tattered tunic. The city was alive, but it didn't give a damn about people like him. You either took what you needed, or you were swallowed whole.

He has a lean, wiry build—built by hunger and hardship. Tanned skin, faint scars, and dark, uneven hair. A face that blended in well. Forgettable.

His clothes were worse. A tunic that used to be blue but now looked like it had lost a war. Trousers held together by sheer willpower. Boots so worn they barely deserved the name.

But his eyes, his eyes were different.

Storm-gray, sharp, always moving. Always watching. Always marking the nearest escape route. They were restless, intelligent—haunted.

Dorian had survived the streets of Mythralis for years, outwitting the city guards, outpacing merchants when he stole food, outmaneuvering other street rats before they stole from him. At sixteen, he was good at exactly one thing: taking what he needed and disappearing before anyone noticed.

Tonight would be no different.

Not just any mark would do. He'd learned that the hard way.

Too poor, and he'd risk his life for a handful of copper. Too rich, and the city guards would hunt him down before he could even spend it. No, what he needed was the sweet spot—someone fat with wealth, but too lazy or distracted to guard it properly. Someone like...

Him.

The merchant's rings glinted in the fading sunlight, fingers plump as he thumbed through a heavy coin pouch. His silks were clean, his boots polished—not a working man, then. Probably a trader, one who made enough gold off his crew's backs to sit comfortably and watch them work.

Dorian smirked. *Perfect.*

He spotted an easy mark—a fat merchant too busy counting his gold to keep an eye on his belt. His focus flickering between his coins and the crates of perfumes and silks being loaded onto his ship. Careless.

Dorian moved. A step. A shift. A brush of fabric. His fingers worked quick, silent, precise. The pouch was gone before the merchant even felt the weight leave his belt.

By the time the fool noticed, Dorian was already in the shadows of a narrow alley, flipping open the soft red velvet pouch.

He leaned against the damp stone wall, letting the shadows swallow him. No shouts. No alarm bells. He was in the clear.

Or so he thought.

A pair of boots stomped past the alley's entrance. Dorian held his breath. The merchant wasn't screaming yet, but that didn't mean a guard hadn't noticed something.

"You hear about the last thief they caught?"

"The one they dragged through the streets?"

"Yeah. Made it all the way to the southern gate before they cut off his hands. Bled out before sunset."

The second guard chuckled. "Better than what happened to the last one. They let the Syndicate have him."

Dorian stayed perfectly still.

The guards moved on.

He let out a slow breath, heart hammering. He needed to get out of here before the merchant noticed what was missing.

"Well, shit," Dorian mutters. Inside are four gold pieces and a few silvers. Enough to keep him fed for a few days—not the haul he'd been hoping for. "This is fucking bullshit," he grumbled under his breath. "That man looked like he'd have at least ten gold pieces, a few silvers, and a couple of coppers. And maybe a ring or two I could pawn."

Dorian huffed and shoved the pouch into his tunic. Just his luck—he risks his neck, and all he gets is a meal plan for the week.

He sighed and slipped into a tavern, the scent of roasted meat and cheap ale filling his lungs. The tavern was packed—dockworkers, merchants, and a handful of mercenaries drowning themselves in cheap ale. A barmaid dodged a drunken grab with practiced ease, slamming a wooden mug in front of a scowling sailor. Dice clattered at a gambling table, followed by a string of curses as a man lost half his earnings.

Dorian kept his head down. He'd learned early that taverns were just as dangerous as the streets. Too many people looking for a fight. Too many desperate men willing to stab someone over a spilled drink.

He took a seat in the back, watching, listening.

Then, an argument near the bar catches his attention.

"I'm tell you; the Eye of Shadows is real!" a bearded man from Seaphos bellowed. "King Theron himself has spent decades searching for it."

"Everyone knows Theron's a fucking madman." grunted a giant of a man from Frostvyrd, resting one hand on the axe at his side.

The name hung in the air like a stormcloud.

The Eye of Shadows.

A dozen sailors subtly adverted their gazes.

Other scoffed, but their laughter was too forced.

Superstition.

Fear.

Dorian had heard the stories before—but now, looking at the expressions around him, he wondered.

Maybe stories had teeth.

Dorian snorted as he rolled his eyes and took a sip of watered-down ale. He'd heard this story a thousand times.

The Eye of Shadows. Rhexion. The dragon that burned entire kingdoms to ash in search of some lost artifact. Just another legend sailors told to keep themselves entertained on long voyages. Just a way for parents to scare their kids into behaving. Dorian had never believed in such stories, for that's all they were. Stories.

The tavern door slammed open like someone had the hounds of hell after them.

"King Haldor's men are in the city!" a man shouted; his breath heavy as if he'd just run a marathon.

The room *froze*.

For one, excruciating heartbeat, the only sound was the crackle of the fireplace. Then, chairs scraped against the floor. Men grabbed their weapons. Conversations turned to hushed whispers.

A tavern-goer near the door swore under his breath and slipped out the back exit. No one stopped him. No one wanted to get caught in the wrong place at the wrong time.

Well, guess Dorian was right about the hounds of hell being after someone. King Haldor's soldiers might as well be hellhounds with how they act and their tendency to stab first, ask questions never.

Dorian didn't move. Didn't react. But his mind sharpened.

Haldor's men *never* came to Mythralis without reason. Unless a few of them just wanted to kill something for fun, which is a possibility Dorian didn't even *want* to think about.

And if there was one thing Dorian had learned, it was this—bad feelings were usually right.

Chapter Two

The Price of Survival

"Power does not corrupt—it reveals what was always hidden."—Elysian Scholar

Dorian left the tavern before the second silence hit.

The kind that comes after the panic.

When the crowd thins. When people stop shouting and start disappearing.

When people with sense go home—and people like him vanish.

Haldor's men were in Mythralis.

That was not routine. That wasn't a patrol.

That was a problem.

He pulled his hood up as he slipped into the streets, the last glow of the tavern fire flickering against the back of his boots.

He didn't run. Not yet. Running would draw eyes.

But he moved.

Not toward home—he didn't have one.

Not toward familiar corners—he didn't want to lead a trail.

Instead, he took the long way around. Through the back alleys and rotten merchant paths, where buildings leaned too close and no one asked questions.

The night air had a bite to it. Not cold. Just sharp.

The kind of sharp that made your instincts twitch.

He slipped past shuttered windows, beneath drying laundry still hanging between buildings like prayer flags. Somewhere, a dog barked. Somewhere else, someone screamed—but no one answered.

Mythralis was starting to notice something was off.

And Dorian noticed Mythralis.

He knew what it looked like when a city braced for something ugly.

Shops that were open a few minutes ago were now locked up tight. Shadows loomed behind curtained windows. The laughter from the tavern was gone.

People were waiting.

For something.

Dorian didn't wait.

He dropped into a narrow cut between buildings, feet landing silent on old cobblestone, then turned down another alley, then another—moving like someone who'd done this dance a hundred times. Because he had.

He'd survived Mythralis his whole life not by being strong—but by being gone before the blow landed.

And Haldor's men didn't come to ask questions.

They came to burn things down.

He remembered the stories. Cities they'd marched through. People they'd "cleansed." Families that went missing. Their presence always meant someone had whispered the wrong name, stolen the wrong coin, looked the wrong direction.

He glanced over his shoulder.

Still no sound.

Still no footsteps.

Still not safe.

He slipped into a tight corridor that ran behind a butcher's row—filthy, stinking, half-lit by a flickering lantern—and paused to listen.

Then he heard it.

The first whistle.

Short. Sharp. Military.

One call.

A few heartbeats later—another. Farther left. Answering.

He froze.

They were triangulating.

Not guards. Not Syndicate. Soldiers.

He didn't know if they were after him. Not yet.

But it didn't matter.

He'd stolen from the wrong person. Asked the wrong question. Or maybe they'd just decided tonight was a good night to kill someone like him.

Dorian's pulse kicked.

He exhaled once through his nose.

Just once.

Then he was moving again.

Down the corridor. Over a stone wall. Across a rain-slicked rooftop. Boots whispering on tile, cloak snapping behind him like a warning.

His breath curled in the air.

Too fast.

Too loud.

He ducked into an old apothecary—boarded up and forgotten—and slipped through a broken grate in the back wall. His body slid into the passage with the ease of someone who had memorized every crack in this part of the city.

Below him—darkness.

Tunnels.

The old city. The buried one. Forgotten and dangerous.

But not as dangerous as what was coming.

He dropped in, silent.

And as he disappeared into the tunnels, the shouts started above.

Not close.

But not far.

Just enough to mean they'd found something. Or someone. Or maybe him.

He didn't wait to find out.

Because in Mythralis, hesitation had a price.

And tonight, survival might cost more than he had left to pay.

And somewhere behind him, the first footfalls echoed in the dark.

Chapter Three

The Oracle's Prophecy

"Mercy is a tactic. Vengeance is a strategy."—Stormrheim Codex

☐

Dorian ran.

He knew what happened to street rats caught by King Haldor's men. They didn't get fucking warnings. They didn't get trials like everyone else. They got executed, which is something that is not on Dorian's to-do list.

The tunnels twisted around him, uneven stone threatening to trip him with every step. His breath came fast, burning his lungs, but he did not slow down.

Behind him—the clang of armored boots.

Too close. Too fucking close.

Dorian risked a glance back. A mistake.

A flash of metal—a crossbow bolt slammed into the stone inches from his shoulder. Splinters of rock scraped his cheek, but he didn't stop.

"There! I see him!"

Shit.

He ducked low, heart hammering, pushing himself harder. His legs burned, lungs raw, but the tunnel twisted ahead, offering a chance, a way out—

If he could make it.

Dorian turned sharply, nearly losing his footing on the damp stone. The tunnel widened, opening into an ancient chamber hidden beneath Mythralis. The air changed.

Colder. Stiller. The scent of damp stone and something older—dust, decay, and a faint metallic tang, like blood long dried.

Massive pillars loomed from the darkness, their surfaces worn with age, carved symbols he didn't recognize. The remains of statues stood against the walls—some missing heads, others crumbled entirely. It felt like a place that had been forgotten, buried beneath the weight of time itself.

Dorian swallowed hard. Whatever this place was, it wasn't just ruins. It was a tomb.

And then he saw her.

A woman—collapsed against the wall, breathing in ragged, shallow gasps. Strange symbols flickered across her skin, glowing faintly in the dim light. Her robes were torn, blood soaking through the fabric.

She barely looked alive.

Dorian's instincts screamed at him to keep moving. To get the fuck out of here.

But he hesitated.

Because the woman wasn't just bleeding—she was glowing. Strange symbols flickered across her skin, a language he didn't know but somehow felt carved into his bones.

She was dying. That much was obvious. But something about her felt... wrong. Not wrong like dangerous. Wrong like fate twisting itself into knots, pulling him toward something he had no touching.

And yet, his feet moved forward. One step. Then another.

Like he had a choice.

Dorian cursed under his breath. He did not have time to deal with this shit when he had soldiers after him.

Dorian hesitated. One step forward. Then another.

She grabbed his wrist.

Heat flared where her fingers touched him—searing, unnatural. Dorian sucked in a sharp breath, but his vision blurred, his thoughts fracturing into something vast and terrible.

"The Eye awakens."

Pain tore through his forearm, whit-hot and blinding. He gasped, jerking back, but her grip held like iron. Symbols—the same glowing symbols—burned into his flesh.

Fire. Shadow. A dragon's eye snapped open in the abyss.

Not just an eye. A presence.

Massive. Ancient. Watching.

Dorian couldn't move—no, he wasn't even himself anymore. He was somewhere else, somewhere burning. Flames roared around him, consuming cities, turning stone to molten ruin. Screams filled the air.

And through it all, that eye.

It saw him.

A single breath rumbled through the void, deep as the earth itself. Then a whisper, curling through the flames like a smoke—not a voice, but a promise.

"Awaken."

Dorian snapped back to reality, gasping.

The words weren't just spoken—they were etched into reality itself.

Grooms   Eye of Shadows

They burned through him, searing into his bone, his mind, his soul. Old words. Heavy words.

The voice was neither kind nor cruel.

It simply was.

And then—words, ancient and absolute, filled his mind.

"When the Eye is lost and the storm is nigh,

Shadow shall wake and kingdoms shall die.

The god-born rise, the dragons call,

Yet one stands alone, the key to all.

In fire and frost, in light and dark,

The world shall break with fate's first spark.

A child of men, bound by thread,

Shall walk where gods and dragons tread.

Raevnir blood and dragon's flame

Shall shape the war, yet none remain.

For what was forged in night's embrace,

Shall end or damn the elder race.

Seek they Eye before the fall,

For he who claims shall rule them all.

Yet beware the cost of Shadow's sight—

For in his gaze, the end ignites."

And then—she was gone.

Not dead. Gone.

Her body collapsed into dust.

Like she had never been there at all.

But the dust... it lingered. Swirling in the air like embers from a dying fire, drifting towards Dorian, clinging to his skin.

His arm still burned. The symbols still glowed.

The silence pressed around him, thick and suffocating. Like the world had been holding its breath—and had just decided to exhale.

Dorian staggered back, clutching his arm. The symbols still burned.

Dorian barely had time to catch to catch his breath, to process the impossible fucking nightmare that had just happened.

Then he heard it.

A blade sliding from a sheath.

Footsteps—multiple, moving fast.

"There! In the ruins!"

Dorian's stomach dropped. Not now. Not after that.

But the universe, as always, was a cruel bastard.

The soldiers had found him.

And they were not coming to take him alive.

Grooms   Eye of Shadows

Chapter Four

Hunted By Shadows

"Shadow follows light not out of envy, but out of loyalty."—Teachings of the First Raevnir

☐

Dorian sprinted through the tunnels.

A dead end.

His stomach dropped as he skidded to a stop. The walls of the chamber rose high—smooth, impossible to climb.

Nowhere to run.

The soldiers were closing in.

Boots pounded against the stone behind him, their rhythmic clang bouncing off the tunnel walls. Dorian didn't look back—looking back was how you fucking died.

"Spread out!" a voice barked. "Cut him off!"

Dorian clenched his jaw. That wasn't good.

A sharp whistle cut through the air—a signal. Then a second one, coming from up ahead.

His stomach dropped. They weren't just chasing him. They were herding him.

"Shit," he muttered under his breath, pushing himself faster. His legs burned. His breath came in sharp bursts, but he didn't stop. Couldn't stop.

The tunnel narrowed, sloping downward. He nearly lost his footing on the slick stone, arms flailing before he caught himself against the rough wall. If he didn't find a way out fast, he was dead.

Then—movement in the shadows.

A figure stepped forward, slipping out of the darkness like a whisper of smoke. Cloaked in black, hood titled just slightly enough to be infuriatingly annoying, standing too still. Too calm.

"Well, aren't you in a spectacular amount of trouble?"

Dorian stared. The figure stood there, relaxed, arms crossed, like he had all the time in the world. Cloaked in black, just enough of his face visible to be smug about it.

Dorian narrowed his eyes. "Who the fuck are you?"

The figure let out a long, exaggerated sigh. "Stars, save me, you're one of those difficult ones aren't you?"

Dorian did not move. His fingers twitched toward the dull dagger at his hip. It wouldn't do any good, but one could certainly hope. "Oh, I'm sorry. Did you expect a 'thank you, mysterious hooded bastard'?"

"Would've been nice," Veranis muttered. "But no, instead I get the sarcastic stray Velocia warned me about."

Dorian scowled, his hand now resting fully on the hilt of his dagger. "Still not an answer."

"And yet, here we are." Veranis sighed, as if rescuing him was a massive inconvenience. "Of course, Velocia would send me to pick up a street wise, untrusting kid. Because why wouldn't she? Not like I have anything better to do with my time." Veranis mutters before turning back towards Dorian. "Name's Veranis. And since you're about to be run through by half of Haldor's men, you should probably start moving. Unless you want to be skewered like a shish kebab, then by all means, stay put."

Dorian frowned. "Right. And I'm supposed to just follow you?"

Veranis stepped forward. Too fast.

Before Dorian could react, they grabbed his wrist.

Electricity shot through him—no, not electricity. Something older. Wilder.

Dorian sucked in a sharp breath, but it felt like his lungs were on fire. The world shattered.

Flames. Darkness.

A roar that wasn't just sound but force, shaking the very bones of the earth. The heat seared his skin, his vision splintering as a massive dragon's eye snapped open in the void.

It saw him.

Dorian's body locked up. Not from fear—from something deeper. Something binding. The eye burned into him, it's gaze a weight, a command, a curse.

Then he was back

His knees buckled. His head pounded. His wrist still burned.

He yanked back, breath sharp and unsteady. "What the hell was that?"

Veranis clicked his tongue. "Oh, you know. Just the weight of destiny and impending doom settling into your bones. No biggie."

Dorian's glare could have melted stone. "You want to try again with a real answer?"

Veranis smirked, his serrated fangs glinting slightly. "Alright, fine. You've been marked. That means the Syndicate, the soldiers, and every other nightmare in the dark will be hunting you now. Congratulations. You're officially the most important person on everyone's 'wanted' list."

Dorian dragged a hand down his face as he groaned, "fantastic."

Before Veranis could add another sarcastic remark, the ground shook.

The air shifted.

Not just cold—unnatural. The kind of cold that sank into bone, into marrow, hollowing you out from the inside.

Dorian exhaled, and his breath came out in a cloud of frost.

Then he heard it.

A deep, rumbling exhale curled through the darkness like ice on the winter winds. Slow, deliberate, vibrating through the stone beneath his feet.

Something moved in the darkness.

Dorian's body locked up as a shadow unfolded from the ruins ahead, massive and glacial, scales catching the faintest sliver of light.

Then—eyes.

Not human. Not mortal. Slit-pupiled, molten amber, staring straight at him.

The temperature dropped as ice began to slither in across the stone floor like frozen fractals, creeping towards them.

The ice slithered across the stone faster now. Reaching. Consuming. The air sharpened, biting into his skin.

Veranis muttered something under his breath that Dorian was pretty sure was some kind of 'fuck me' equivalent in another language.

"Oh, for fuck's sake. Of course it's Cryos." His voice was sharp now but not panicked. If anything, he sounded annoyed.

"As in the dragon?" Dorian demanded.

"No, as in the pastry chef. Of course it's the dragon!" Veranis threw him a flat look. "Massive son of a bitch. Nasty too. Breathes ice. Hates people. Probably going to eat you. That clear enough?"

Dorian gawked at him. "That is not helpful."

"Neither is standing there while he decides if you're a snack," Veranis shot back.

Dorian ran a hand down his face. "You know, for someone rescuing me, you're really fucking annoying."

Veranis grinned, his serrated fanged upper canines once again flashing. "It's a gift."

Dorian groaned. "Why are you like this?"

"Born this way. Now shut up and move."

Veranis grabbed Dorian's arm and dragged him into motion. "Move, street rat. If the soldiers, the Syndicate, or Cryos catches you, you're dead."

Dorian didn't argue.

He turned and ran.

Veranis moved ahead, navigating the tunnels with an ease that made Dorian's skin crawl. Veranis wasn't panicking. He wasn't rushing.

He was having fun.

Behind them, Cryos stirred.

Chapter Five

Escape to Elysia

"The battlefield is a temple. Worship wisely."—Aegyptean War Hymns

☐

Dorian was not sure how much longer their battered little boat would hold together.

The azure sea churned violently beneath them, the salt-laden wind whipped against his face like he had personally insulted it. Above, storm clouds gathered in thick, writhing masses, distant streaks of lighting flickering through the darkness.

And behind them—death followed on the waves.

Two ships pursued them, cutting through the waves like hungry leviathans.

The first—the one that made Dorian's stomach knot—bore black sails marked with a crimson sun. The Black Sun Syndicate. The worst kind of killers. They weren't pirates, not in the traditional sense. They were organized, ruthless, and smart. A deck full of mercenaries who didn't kill just for gold—they enjoyed it.

The second ship wasn't much better. Bounty hunters. Armed to the teeth, with grappling hooks already being prepped to drag them in. Which meant someone had put a dangerously high price on Dorian's head.

Wonderful.

Dorian tightened his grip on the railing, scowling. "You wouldn't happen to have some miracle escape plan, would you?"

Veranis stood at the bow, utterly unfazed—which only pissed Dorian off more.

Wind lashed against his golden-blond hair, his massive silver feathered wings folded tight against his back. His emerald-green eyes weren't on their pursuers. They were locked on the storm ahead.

That was never a good sign.

"They're getting closer," Dorian gritted out, trying to steady himself against the wild thrashing of the boat. He'd much rather have his feet on solid ground than this.

Still, no response.

Instead, Veranis lifted a hand, fingers curling like he was pulling at something unseen.

The air around them thickened, pressing down like the weight of an oncoming storm, making it harder to breathe.

Dorian's breath hitched.

His skin crawled.

It wasn't just magic. Magic, he understood—had seen before. But this? This felt like the ocean itself had paused to listen. Like the air was waiting for Veranis's command.

Dorian had spent his life on the streets, learning to read the unspoken rules of survival. And right now, every instinct was screaming—Veranis was not someone to cross.

The sunlight dimmed unnaturally—as if the sun had suddenly decided to fuck off early.

And then—the sea roared like a beast awakening.

Behind them, the ocean rose.

A wave the size of a building surged upward, curling high above the enemy ships before crashing down like the fist of an angry god.

Wood shattered. Sails tore. Men screamed as they were flung into the raging waters below.

Dorian had no idea how many of them were dead, but he wasn't about to complain.

He barely had time to process what had happened before—

A harpoon sliced through the air.

The massive iron spear slammed into their boat with a sickening crack. The force nearly launched Dorian overboard as the entire vessel shuddered violently.

"They're still coming!" He shouted.

Another harpoon whistled through the air.

Dorian saw it too late.

And then—the world broke apart.

Reality ripped away around him.

One moment, he was on the deck, caught in the chaos of the storm. The next—

Nothing.

Dorian was falling.

Not through water. Not through air. Through something else.

The emptiness wasn't just absence—it was living, breathing nothingness.

He couldn't tell if he was moving or if the void itself was moving around him. The edges of his vision flickered—not like darkness, but like something chewing at the seams of existence.

The whispers curled deeper, sliding into his ears, beneath his skin.

Dorian clenched his jaw.

It wasn't just a void. It was watching.

Then—a sudden snap. Like a thread yanked too hard.

And he was somewhere else.

Darkness coiled around him.

Whispers slithered through the void, stroking against his mind. He couldn't make out the words—or maybe he didn't want to. They were old. Ancient. Hungry.

His pulse roared in his ears.

Then—

He slammed back into existence.

Dorian hit the deck hard, gasping.

Pain jolted through his limbs, his muscles twisting like they'd been stretched and compressed all at once.

His heart pounded violently. His skin burned where the glowing symbols on his arm pulsed, alive with energy that didn't belong to him.

His stomach lurched. He rolled to the side, barely avoiding face-planting into a coil of rope, and forced himself upright. Everything was spinning.

"What the fuck was that?" He wheezed.

Veranis, of course, is completely unbothered.

"Dimensional slip," he said, brushing sea spray from his sleeve like they weren't actively being hunted. "Rather unpleasant, I imagine. You'll get used to it."

Dorian glared at him. "Used to it? *Used to it*?! You *ripped* reality apart and threw me through some kind of hell-void, and I'm supposed to get *used to it*?!"

Veranis smirked, because he was an insufferable bastard.

"Yes," he said simply.

Dorian dragged a shaking hand down his face. "I hate you."

"Good. It'll make this next part even more fun."

Dorian didn't like the sound of that.

Then—another harpoon flew straight at them.

Dorian's body moved on instinct. He threw himself sideways as the harpoon slammed into the deck, punching straight through the wood.

The boat was falling apart. If they took another hit, they were done.

He grabbed the railing, shoving himself up, trying to force his dizzying vision to focus.

Behind them, the Syndicate ship was still afloat—damaged, but afloat. The bounty hunters had pulled back slightly, trying to avoid the wreckage caused by Veranis's wave, but they were already reloading another harpoon.

"We need a new plan!" Dorian shouted.

Veranis just smirked. "I have one."

Veranis extended his hand again.

This time, the shadows around them rippled.

The boat lurched violently. Dorian grabbed onto the mast, cursing as the wood creaked under the strain of something unnatural.

The air fractured.

It didn't feel like teleporting—it felt like the world itself was tearing apart.

The mast groaned. The sea blurred. Dorian's breath hitched as the edges of reality rippled and folded inward, like pages of a book being rewritten.

The sky darkened.

Not from clouds. From something else.

And then—

They were gone as everything vanished.

Chapter Six

The Gods Take Notice

"Truth bends to survival, as iron bends to flame."—Elysian Scholar

Verdant Haven was alive around her—the towering silverwood trees glowed faintly in the twilight, their leaves shimmering like woven starlight. The air was thick with ancient power, old as the first breath of the world itself. Fireflies flickered in the shadows, their golden light pulsing in rhythm with something deeper—the heartbeat of the land.

She had felt it.

The balance of power had shifted—something ancient was stirring, something long thought lost.

The land whispered its warnings, but only those who listened could hear. Velocia had lived through ages, watched civilizations rise and crumble like sandcastles beneath the tide.

Yet this... this felt different.

Not just a shift. A reckoning.

And the gods were moving. That alone was reason to be wary.

And now, she had to deal with her children.

She gathered Aetherion, Varyn, and Niran before her.

Aetherion held himself like a warrior waiting for battle, his storm-blue gaze flickering with barely contained tension. His pale blond hair was tousled by the wind, his black-feathered wings gleaming silver in the fading light.

Varyn, ever the opportunist, smirked as if he were already two steps ahead of whatever scheme he was forming. He was all sharp grins and relaxed confidence, leaning lazily against a tree, arms crossed, his silver wings flicking absently. His charcoal-gray hair fell messily over his forehead, half-intentional, half just how he was. But his amber eyes—those burned with something deeper. Something he didn't often show.

And Niran?

He was pacing. Like a caged fire, like he'd rather tear through the sky than stand still.

The menace. The wildfire.

His red hair was windswept and tangled, a reflection of his energy. His vivid blue eyes glinted with mischief, and his wings—brilliant flames of red, orange, and gold—never seemed to settle. Always shifting, always moving.

Velocia exhaled slowly. She loved her sons. She did. But gods above, they tested her patience.

"The Eye of Shadows has awakened," she said, her voice even, steady.

The words settled over them like an oncoming storm. The air thickened. Even the silverwood trees, ancient and wise, seemed to hush their glowing whispers.

Aetherion stiffened. Varyn's smirk faded. Niran stopped pacing.

Aetherion inhaled sharply. "That's a myth."

Velocia's expression did not change. "No. It is a warning. Loki and Gaia are moving. They seek the Eye for their own ends."

Niran and Varyn exchanged a glance. Oh no. That was never a good sign.

"And what exactly do you expect us to do?" Varyn asked, stretching his arms. "Because I, for one, am not in the mood for divine bullshit."

Niran leaned closer, eyes gleaming. "I mean, if we're talking divine bullshit, I'd at least like an incentive. A kingdom? A dragon's hoard? Immortality?"

Varyn snorted. "You already have immortality, idiot."

"Fine, then I want a kingdom."

"You'd burn it down within a week."

Niran grinned. "Exactly."

Velocia leveled him with a look. "Watch. Listen. The boy—Dorian—is more important than you realize."

Niran let out a low whistle. "So we're babysitting a human?"

Aetherion frowned. "If Loki and Gaia are involved, it's more than that."

Niran turned to Varyn, grinning. "You think we're getting paid for this?"

Varyn smirked. "Oh, absolutely not."

Velocia pinched the bridge of her nose. "If you two are done acting like idiots—"

"Oh, Mother, please." Niran flashed an innocent smile. "Acting implies effort."

Aetherion sighed. Varyn grinned.

Velocia stared at them both.

"I should've left you in the void when I had the chance."

Velocia had faced ancient horrors, stared into the abyss, and walked unscathed from wars that shattered realms—yet somehow, nothing tested her patience quite like her own sons.

Far beyond Verdant Haven, the earth cracked beneath heavy footsteps.

Two figures stood at the edge of the volcanic wastelands, watching the world shift around them.

Kael was a mountain of shadow and fire. His obsidian-black scales gleamed like polished onyx, and the heat from his body warped the air itself. His wings, tipped in copper and molten red, stretched wide, shimmering like living metal beneath the fractured sky.

His crystalline blue eyes were cold. Calculating. A predator who had never known fear.

Beside him, Aurora stood like the night sky itself had been given form.

Her luminous scales shifted between emerald, cerulean, and violet, a living aurora borealis. Her wings, spanning 130 feet, draped behind her like a celestial cloak, woven from pure starlight. Her opal-green eyes flickered with something unreadable—wisdom, power, and something untamed.

Kael exhaled slowly, his fangs glinting in the firelight.

"It has begun."

The earth groaned beneath Kael's weight. Molten veins of lava cracked and pulsed under his claws, the wasteland shifting restlessly around him—as if even the land itself feared what was coming.

Aurora's feathers flared, catching the faint celestial glow in the sky.

"Then we must find him before they do."

Lightning flashed in the distance.

Kael's tail flicked against the ground, sending cracks through the hardened lava beneath him.

"He carries the mark," Kael murmured.

Aurora didn't look away from the horizon. "And that means every god and monster will be hunting him."

Kael's claws dug into the stone.

"Then we had better move quickly."

The storm raged on.

And somewhere, beyond the shattered sky, something watched. Something that had waited far too long.

Chapter Seven

The Blood of a God

"Only the dead understand the price of silence."—Stormrheim Codex

The fire crackled in slow rhythms as twilight fell across Verdant Haven.

Velocia stood just outside the glow, half-shadowed beneath the silverwood trees. She watched her sons spar in the clearing—blades flashing, wings slicing the dusk like ribbons of flame and night.

Varyn laughed as he flipped away from Niran's strike, cocky and sharp as always. Niran's reply came in a flurry of heat and motion, sparks trailing from his fists.

Aetherion didn't speak. Didn't grin.

He moved like a storm learning patience.

His blade didn't scream like theirs—it whispered. A silver edge sliding through air with deadly grace. Precision born of control. Of command.

There was something in the way he turned—shoulders square, jaw tight, gaze steady—that made her chest seize.

Zeus.

She saw it for just a breath.

The way his stance commanded the ground.

The way his voice, when he gave a clipped instruction to his younger brothers, carried authority. The stillness. The cold fire.

It was a fragment. But it was enough.

The air in her lungs turned razor-thin. Her fingers curled. Her heart stumbled in her chest.

And then—

She wasn't in the clearing anymore.

Cold stone slammed back into her knees.

Divine shackles snapped around her wrists.

The scent of Olympus rose like rot—jasmine, ash, and lightning.

Her body remembered it before her mind could scream.

Her breath came in ragged gasps, her body trembling under the weight of their latest round. The sigils burned against her skin. The walls whispered—voices of the forgotten, the damned—echoing the vast emptiness of her prison.

Zeus loomed over her, golden and smug and reeking of conquest. His expression was satisfied, like a king admiring a city razed to dust.

Velocia hated this.

Hated that, despite being a goddess of creation, she had been reduced to property.

He withdrew with slow arrogance, his hand sliding down her bare spine like he owned her.

"You're strong," he said, breath still heavy. "I always liked that about you."

She didn't speak. Couldn't.

Her mouth was split. Her jaw dislocated. Blood filled the back of her throat.

Ares leaned against the nearest pillar, arms crossed and smiling with teeth. Heracles flipped a coin beside him, disinterested but waiting for his turn.

Loki stood in the shadows, half-shrouded, silver eyes gleaming with something unspoken.

He didn't move toward her.

Not yet.

Zeus's voice curled around her like smoke.

"You'll thank me one day."

He left without waiting for an answer.

The silence that followed wasn't silence.

It was tension. Waiting. A breath held by the universe.

Then Loki stepped forward.

She didn't look at him. But she knew that scent. That careful way he walked. That voice.

"You will break, little goddess."

Velocia clenched her jaw. Blood dripped from her fingertips.

"Try me."

Her indigo-blue wings flared wide, feathers shimmering with star-born light. Torn. Bloodied. Celestial.

"I refuse to break. And I will fly once more."

"You were magnificent once," Loki said, his voice almost tender. "Now look at you. Chained. Broken. Bleeding. Tell me… how long will that fire of yours last?"

She didn't answer.

Because she felt it.

Something different. Something new.

Her body ached in strange places. Her magic had shifted. Bent. Changed.

She was pregnant.

She knew it like she knew her name.

No… not yet. Please—not yet.

She was shaking. But she wasn't crying.

She wouldn't give them that.

Loki crouched in front of her. "You'll understand in time. You were never meant to be free, Velocia. You were meant to be a vessel."

He touched her stomach.

That was when she snapped.

She lunged forward, teeth bared, and bit him—ripped a line down his wrist that would never fully heal.

He didn't strike her.

He smiled.

And walked away.

She remembered the way her wings wrapped around her body in the months that followed. How she refused to speak to anyone. How the stars whispered lullabies to her belly because she wouldn't.

Aetherion was born in silence.

She hadn't screamed. Hadn't wept.

Just held him in her arms, staring down into eyes that mirrored the storm she had once tried to command.

He didn't cry.

He just looked up at her like he already knew what the world was.

Her firstborn.

The product of a nightmare.

And still—she loved him.

Not because she should. Not because she chose him.

But because despite it all—he was hers.

And the gods would never have him.

Velocia gasped.

Reality hit like a slap.

She was back beneath the silverwoods. The clearing was quiet now—her sons had stopped. Varyn was laughing. Niran was groaning. Aetherion stood a little apart, sword resting against his shoulder, gaze fixed on the horizon.

He didn't see her watching him.

Didn't know what he was.

Didn't know who had made him.

But one day—he would.

And on that day, when the storm of Zeus's

blood tried to rise inside him—

She would be there.

To remind him that he was not his father's son.

He was hers.

And the world would kneel to that.

Chapter Eight

Secrets in Sylvaria

"To walk between stars is to carry both burden and blessing."—The teachings of the First Raevnir

Dorian hated this. Every step felt like a battle. The mountain winds cut like knives, icy and relentless, biting into his skin even through his tattered clothes. The wind didn't just cut—it carved. His fingers were numb. His lungs burned. His legs ached from climbing over jagged rock, and the cold gnawed at his bones. His boots—if they could still be called that—were a disaster, the soles barely cling together as he trudged over uneven stone.

He wasn't sure what was worse—the mountain trying to kill him, or Veranis being an insufferable cryptic bastard.

And worst of all—Veranis moved like a storm given form

Veranis was still refusing to answer his damn questions.

"You're not just human," Veranis had said.

Over. And over.

Dorian's patience was nonexistent at this point.

"No shit," he snapped, pulling his cloak tighter around him. "That doesn't actually tell me anything."

Veranis, of course, was as unbothered as ever. The bastard wasn't even shivering, standing there with his usual smug look of mystery and menace.

They had finally arrived at Sylvania, the mountain city of Elysia, where—if Veranis wasn't bullshitting him—ancient texts might finally give him some damn answers.

The Temple of the Fates loomed ahead, its marble pillars cracked with age, yet untouched by time. The air felt different here, charged with something unseen, something waiting.

Dorian paused. His instincts screamed at him.

Something was wrong.

The air inside wasn't just heavy—it was expectant. The walls whispered in a language he couldn't quite hear, something just beneath the edge of understanding. The stone was cold under his fingertips, but the altar pulsed with a strange warmth.

Like it recognized him.

"You feel it, don't you?" Veranis murmured.

Dorian did.

The moment he stepped inside, the world tilted.

A whisper curled around his mind, soft but insistent.

And then—

The visions struck.

Fire. A hunger that could never be satisfied.

A dragon's eye, molten gold, seething with something ancient. Watching him. Seeing through him.

A hand—his hand—reaching, desperate grasping at something just out of reach. A name, slipping from his tongue like smoke.

The world cracked apart.

Pain seared through his veins, his skin burning as the symbols on his arm pulsed—alive, screaming.

Dorian staggered, gripping the edge of an altar to stay upright.

Priests moved around them, their robes whispering against the cold marble floors. Their eyes gleamed with knowing, their expressions unreadable.

"The Eye has been lost since Rhexion's fall," one of them murmured. "But its power stirs once more."

Dorian's heart was still racing. He didn't know what any of this meant—

But he had a feeling he was about to find out.

Because outside—

Something was coming.

The priests had gone still. No murmured prayers. No whispered conversations.

Just silence.

A terrible, waiting silence.

And then—

A scream.

A shadow fell over the temple.

The sound of shouts, weapons clashing—then a scream.

Dorian spun, pulse hammering.

Outside the temple, the city was erupting into chaos.

And then—

The doors burst open.

Figures poured in—black-cloaked warriors, blades gleaming like moonlight on steel.

The Syndicate.

Dorian's blood went cold.

Veranis didn't hesitate.

His dagger was already in his hand, silver wings flaring wide, shadows curling around his fingertips like living things.

"You might want to move, street rat."

Dorian barely had time to react before the first assassin lunged.

The world exploded into movement.

Dorian barely dodged as a sword whistled past his face, carving deep into the altar beside him. Marble splintered, shards flying.

He hit the ground hard, rolling just as a second assassin lunged—only to be intercepted by Veranis.

Blades clashed in a blur of motion.

Veranis fought like a storm given form, his movements fluid, effortless, deadly. His dagger found its mark between ribs, twisting, dropping one attacker before pivoting to block another strike.

Dorian scrambled back to his feet—just in time for someone to slam into him.

He hit the floor again, breath leaving his lungs in a sharp wheeze as a Syndicate assassin pinned him down, dagger raised.

Dorian didn't think.

He reacted.

His hand shot out, grabbing the wrist holding the dagger. The assassin snarled, forcing it down.

Dorian's mark flared.

It wasn't just power. It was something deeper.

Older.

It burned, but it wasn't fire. It roared through his veins like a storm barely restrained.

The assassin convulsed, body rigid, mouth open in a silent scream—before something unseen *ripped* them away, slamming them against the wall.

Dorian gasped, staring at his own hands.

The air around them still shimmered, warping like heat rising from the stone.

A pulse of something unseen.

What the fuck was that?

No time to think. Another assassin was already charging him.

Veranis's voice cut through the chaos. "You are painfully slow, you know that?"

Dorian had no idea where the hell Veranis was, but he was too busy not dying to snap back at him.

The temple was drenched in chaos.

One of the priests lay dead, his blood soaking into the marble. Others were fighting back, wielding staffs glowing with faint energy—but the Syndicate warriors were relentless.

Dorian ducked another blade, twisting just in time to slam his elbow into an attacker's ribs. They stumbled, but didn't fall.

Dorian's mind raced.

He was outnumbered.

Out armed.

And then the temple shook.

Veranis moved—faster than Dorian had ever seen—striking the ground with his palm.

Shadows rippled outward, curling up like living things—tendrils of darkness lashing out.

The Syndicate warriors recoiled.

But not for long.

Because outside—

Something else was coming.

Dorian felt it before he saw it.

A presence. A force.

Not the Syndicate. Something worse.

And then—

A massive blast of light exploded through the temple doors.

Dorian threw up an arm to shield his eyes as a voice, low and cold, echoing through the hall.

"Enough."

The dust settled.

The very air *shrank* around him. The torches dimmed, shadows bending toward him like supplicants before a god.

The runes etched into his armor *hummed*, shifting, twisting—alive.

Power clung to him, thick as smoke.

And standing in the ruins of the temple doors—

Was someone Dorian had never seen before.

A tall figure, wrapped in armor darker than night, runes etched into the metal like cracks in reality itself. His eyes—burning silver, void-like.

He didn't move like a man.

Too still. Too precise.

The torches flickered in his wake, not from wind, but from something deeper—like the air itself recoiled from him. His silver eyes weren't just bright—they burned. Not with light, but with something else. Something ancient.

Dorian's instincts screamed.

Who the fuck was this?

Veranis's expression finally lost some of its arrogance.

"Ah," he murmured. "Well, that complicates things."

He was never rattled. Never caught off guard.

But now?

His grip on his dagger had *tightened.* His silver wings flicked, tense. A fraction of hesitation. And Dorian didn't like what that meant.

Dorian's stomach dropped.

If Veranis was worried—they were completely fucked.

Chapter Nine

Training in Aresia

"Victory is not the end of war—only its most convincing lie."—Aegyptean War Hymns

☐

Dorian didn't move.

He wasn't sure if he even could.

The silver-eyed figure stood motionless, a specter of death wrapped in runed armor so dark it looked like it had been carved from the void itself. The air around him crackled, thick with something old and heavy. Something wrong.

Every instinct in Dorian's body screamed danger.

The air itself recoiled from him. The torches lining the temple walls flickered—not from wind, but as if something was *devouring the light.*

Hia armor wasn't just black—it seemed to *drink in the surrounding shadows*, a void wrapped in steel.

And those silver eyes—*not human, not mortal.* A depthless, hollow thing. Calculating. Dorian felt like he had already been *measured, weighed, and found lacking.*

Veranis, for once, wasn't smirking.

And that was really fucking bad.

"Ah," Veranis murmured, his voice almost casual, but his posture had shifted—just slightly. His hand hovered over the dagger at his hip. "Well, that complicates things."

Dorian's pulse roared in his ears.

The figure tilted his head, his silver eyes narrowing as he focused entirely on Dorian.

No. Not just focused. Measuring him.

Dorian's fingers twitched toward his dagger. He wasn't stupid—he knew that wouldn't do much against a fully armored warrior, but doing nothing felt even worse.

The stranger took a slow step forward.

Then another.

Veranis shifted. "Yeah, we're not doing this today."

And then—the world split apart again.

Shadows rippled outward, a pulse of power that sent Dorian's stomach twisting.

The temple *fractured* around him, reality splitting like shattered glass.

Dorian's stomach *lurched violently* as the world *twisting inside out*. His body felt both too light and unbearably heavy at the same time.

For a split second—he was nowhere.

Then—

He hit ground, hard, the impact knocking the breath from his lungs.

And when the world snapped back into place—

Dorian was standing somewhere else.

Dorian's head was still spinning when he hit solid ground again.

The moment he steadied himself, his first thought was what the actual fuck just happened?

His second thought was oh, great. More people staring at me.

The warriors of Aresia were *nothing like the cutthroats and mercenaries* Dorian was used to seeing in Mythralis.

They moved like *living weapons*, their gazes sharp, their postures coiled for violence. *Trained killers. Disciplined. Deadly.*

And all of them were looking at *him*.

Judging.

The warrior training grounds of Aresia stretched before him—a massive arena of stone and sand. The banners lining the arena walls bore emblems of noble houses—some he recognized, most he didn't.

The warriors of Aresia weren't just from Elysia. Some hailed from farther lands—Seaphos, Frostvyrd, even the empire of Raevnir itself. If he had any doubts about being out of depth before, they were gone now.

Dorian took one glance around and immediately decided—

He did not belong here.

And judging by the looks he was getting from Aetherion, Varyn, and Niran, they agreed.

Varyn was watching him with that usual sharp glint in his amber eyes, arms crossed as he leaned against a stone pillar. His silver wings flicked slightly, restless.

Niran, on the other hand, looked amused. His fiery wings twitched as he grinned, his entire posture radiating unholy levels of mischief.

"You sure you're ready for this, street rat?"

Dorian scowled. "I'll be fine."

He was absolutely not fine.

Especially not when Aetherion stepped forward and drew his sword.

The blade caught the sunlight, gleaming like liquid silver.

"We'll see about that," Aetherion said, his voice cool and unreadable. He shifted into a ready stance—a stance that screamed trained killer.

Dorian swallowed hard.

Off to the side, Veranis looked far too entertained.

"Try not to die," he offered helpfully.

Dorian barely had time to glare at him before Aetherion moved.

Fast. Too fast.

Dorian barely saw the blade before it was already too late.

Not just speed—precision. Efficiency. The kind of movement that came from years of training. Years of killing.

Aetherion wasn't just testing him. He was showing the difference between them.

He tried to counter—swinging his dagger upward in a desperate strike—

But Aetherion deflected it effortlessly.

Aetherion didn't just dodge—he anticipated. Calculated.

His footwork was too efficient, too clean, as if he had already played through the fight a hundred times in his head before Dorian had even moved.

The impact sent Dorian reeling. He hit the ground hard, skidding across the arena floor.

"Too slow," Aetherion said, not even out of breath.

Dorian gritted his teeth. Yes, no shit.

He pushed himself up just in time to see Aetherion already closing the distance again.

Dorian moved on instinct.

He ducked, rolled—barely avoided a second strike. But Aetherion wasn't letting up.

Another strike. Another near miss.

Dorian needed an opening.

Aetherion's sword came down in a clean, precise arc—

And then—

The air rippled.

The world tilted.

It wasn't just movement—it was like the universe had skipped forward without him.

One second, he was standing in front of Aetherion. The next—

He was somewhere else. Wrong. Out of place. The ground beneath him felt unsteady, like reality itself had barely caught up.

He blinked— and suddenly, he was behind Aetherion. Mid-step. Like the world had just skipped a frame.

Aetherion turned, his sharp blue eyes widening slightly.

The training grounds fell silent.

Dorian's stomach lurched.

What the fuck was that?

He barely had time to process what had just happened before Veranis burst out laughing.

"Well," he said, grinning like a bastard. "That's new."

Before Dorian could figure out whether he was about to pass out or throw up, a new voice cut through the arena.

"Enough."

Dorian turned, still breathing hard, heart pounding.

Velocia was standing on the arena steps, watching him with sharp, calculating amber eyes. Her indigo-feathered wings shifted slightly, the constellation-like pattern across them shimmering.

The air changed the moment she spoke. Not loud. Not forceful.

But absolute.

Every warrior in the arena stood straighter at her presence. Even Aetherion's grip on his sword relaxed slightly.

Dorian didn't know who Velocia was. But he knew, instinctively, that this was not someone you defied.

Veranis stepped forward towards Velocia. He gives her a quick kiss before smirking. "Come to enjoy the show, love?"

Dorian stared. His brain was trying to process this added information.

Velocia chuckled lightly, shaking her head, before turning her attention towards Dorian.

Velocia studied him.

"You have no idea what you just did, do you?"

Dorian scowled, still feeling like his insides had been twisted. "No. But I'm guessing you do?"

Velocia didn't answer immediately.

Instead, she looked at Aetherion, Varyn, and Niran—her sons.

Then at Veranis, her mate.

Then, finally, back at Dorian.

Her next words changed everything.

"That was not magic, Dorian. That was blood."

Blood.

The word coiled around his ribs, sinking deep. Not magic. This wasn't just some accidental surge of power. Not something he could ignore.

This was who he was.

A weight settled in his chest—heavy, suffocating. The same weight he had felt in the temple, in the tunnels, in the ruins of his old life.

He had always been running.

But you can't outrun your own blood.

Dorian staggered backwards.

"What the hell does that mean?"

Velocia exhaled, her gaze steady.

"It means you are not just marked by fate. You are part of something much older."

Dorian felt like the ground beneath him had just shifted.

Because in that moment, he knew—

Everything he thought he knew about himself had just changed.

Chapter Ten

The First Test

"Knowledge is not illumination. It is kindling."—Elysian Scholar

Dorian's heart was still hammering.

The sparring match was over. But his pulse hadn't settled, and his body still remembered the way the world had shifted beneath his feet.

He had teleported.

Not consciously. Not with intent. It had just… happened.

And everyone in the training grounds had noticed.

Varyn and Niran had recovered first—predictably.

Niran let out a low whistle, grinning like a bastard. "Well. That was dramatic."

Varyn, arms crossed, raised a brow. "Yeah, I'd say that's a neat trick."

Dorian clenched his fists, his breathing still uneven. "I don't even know how I—"

"You didn't do it."

Velocia's voice cut through the air, sharp and certain.

Dorian turned, still feeling like his world was tilting.

Velocia stood at the edge of the training grounds, watching him with those piercing amber eyes. Her wings—indigo, shifting with the pattern of constellations—moved slightly as she stepped forward.

She wasn't just guessing.

She knew something.

Dorian swallowed. "Then what the hell just happened?"

Velocia's gaze didn't waver.

"That was not magic, Dorian. That was blood."

The words lodged in his chest.

His blood.

Not magic. Not fate. Something deeper.

Dorian could feel everyone waiting for an answer. Aetherion's expression had barely changed, but there was something calculating behind his storm-blue eyes. Varyn's usual smirk had faded, and even Niran looked more focused than usual.

Veranis, standing just beside Velocia, wasn't grinning anymore.

Dorian exhaled sharply. "And what exactly does that mean?"

Velocia glanced at Veranis—not just glanced, but a look that carried meaning.

Veranis held her gaze for a moment, then sighed, running a hand through his golden-blond hair.

"It means," he said, "that you have a bloodline that no one thought still existed."

Dorian didn't like the sound of that.

Velocia stepped closer. "You are not just marked by fate, Dorian. You are part of something much older."

Dorian's stomach twisted.

He had suspected—in some small, unspoken part of himself—that he wasn't normal. No one had visions like his. No one saw dragons, gods, and ancient horrors in their dreams.

But hearing it spoken aloud? That was different.

Veranis, as usual, looked entirely too casual about this revelation.

"So," Varyn said, rolling his shoulders, "we're just goanna act like that wasn't a bombshell of an answer?"

Niran shrugged. "I mean, I think we all knew he wasn't normal."

"Doesn't make it less annoying," Varyn muttered.

Dorian dragged a hand down his face. "You know, I'd like one day where I don't get told my entire existence is a cosmic joke."

Velocia sighed, her exasperation clear. "You can sulk later. We have bigger problems."

Aetherion folded his arms. "Kael and Aurora."

Velocia nodded. "They know about the Eye."

The group fell silent.

Dorian wasn't stupid. He didn't know much about Kael and Aurora—but judging by the way everyone reacted to their names, they were not people he wanted coming after him.

Veranis was the first to break the silence.

"Right," he said, rolling his shoulders like they had just been given an extremely inconvenient task. "We should get moving, then."

Aetherion didn't argue. Which meant this was serious.

Dorian exhaled. "Where exactly are we going?"

Velocia's gaze locked onto his.

"The ruins of Eryndor. In Stormheim's frozen north."

A Small Problem – They Need to Leave Immediately

Dorian had exactly three seconds to process this before an explosion rocked the training grounds.

Stone cracked. Dust billowed. A tremor ran through the walls of Aresia like something ancient had just been disturbed.

Dorian stumbled back as debris rained down. His heart jumped into his throat.

"What the fuck—"

Velocia's wings flared wide. "Move."

And Dorian, for once, did not argue.

Because he could feel it.

Something was coming.

Far beyond their sight, Loki watched the board shift.

His fingers drifted idly across the edge of his throne, his silver eyes gleaming in the shadows of Yggdrasil's domain.

The Eye was waking. The players were moving.

He watched as Kael and Aurora began their ascent from the volcanic depths.

Watched as Dorian began to understand just how deeply entwined he was in this game.

Watched as Velocia, unshaken and unwavering, stood at the center of it all.

Loki smiled.

"Let's begin."

And somewhere, in the distance, the world shuddered.

Chapter Eleven

The Quiet Between Storms

"You don't command loyalty. You earn it through scars."—Stormrheim War Codex

They stayed in Aresia longer than planned.

After the explosion. After the shift. After the revelation that Dorian wasn't just touched by fate—he was tangled in something ancient, something divine—there was nowhere else to go. Not right away.

Repairs to the training grounds had begun, but some cracks went deeper than stone.

In the quiet days that followed, Velocia planned. Mapped out the threads of war like she could see the tapestry of destiny unraveling thread by thread. She met with leaders, prepared defenses, whispered to the stars like they'd whisper back.

And Veranis stayed.

Not by her side—but not far from it, either.

He didn't shadow her like a soldier. He didn't hover like a husband afraid of being left behind. He was... present. Anchored. And in moments between decisions, when her voice grew tired or her gaze turned distant, he was there—steady as gravity.

Dorian watched them from a distance.

He didn't mean to.

It just happened.

Veranis would brush a loose strand of hair from Velocia's face without thinking. She would lean into his touch without hesitation. There was something easy between them. Ancient. Like they'd fought battles side by side, bled on the same stone, stood together through storms that would've broken anyone else.

It unsettled Dorian.

Because Veranis didn't seem capable of that kind of warmth.

And yet—there it was. Quiet. Fierce. Real.

Dorian pulled his eyes away.

He wasn't part of that world.

Not yet.

Not really.

Later that evening, the brothers found him sitting alone along the northern wall, legs stretched out, arms resting loosely over his knees.

Aetherion approached first—silent and unshakable.

Then Varyn, leaning against the wall like he owned it.

And Niran, rolling a dagger across his knuckles with a grin that promised chaos.

None of them spoke at first.

Then—

"You're not brooding," Varyn said. "I'm disappointed."

"I can go back to brooding if it helps you sleep," Dorian muttered.

A snort. Niran plopped down beside him. "That's the spirit."

Aetherion sat last, folding into the silence with practiced ease.

It wasn't warm.

Not yet.

But it wasn't cold, either.

They talked about nothing at first. Weather. Training. The fact that someone had apparently set part of the mess hall on fire during lunch.

"I didn't do it," Niran said, far too quickly.

"Didn't say you did," Aetherion replied without blinking.

"Yeah, well. Felt like a good time to be preemptively innocent."

Dorian huffed a laugh despite himself.

Varyn glanced at him. "You get used to this."

Dorian raised a brow. "To what?"

"The noise. The constant bickering. The chaos that follows him like smoke." He nodded toward Niran.

"I'm delightful," Niran said.

"You're exhausting," Aetherion muttered.

They all went quiet again.

But this time, it felt like something had shifted.

Dorian didn't say it aloud—but this? This almost felt like being included.

He hadn't expected that.

Not here.

Not yet.

Footsteps approached, and every instinct in Dorian's body went taut—until he heard the voice.

"Are you lot being sentimental again?"

Veranis stood a few paces away, arms crossed, expression unreadable.

Dorian immediately stiffened.

He didn't move. Didn't speak.

But the shift in his posture was enough for Varyn to notice.

Veranis stepped closer. Niran groaned.

"Are you here to say something cryptic or to make it awkward?"

"I'm capable of both," Veranis said smoothly.

Aetherion stood. Not out of tension—out of habit. Respect, maybe.

"You're really coming with us?" he asked.

Veranis nodded. "Your mother's heading west to meet with an old contact. She asked me to go in her place."

"She trusts you that much?" Dorian asked before he could stop himself.

Veranis didn't look offended.

But he looked at Dorian—really looked. And Dorian felt it like a hook behind the ribs.

"She trusts me with the three people she cares about most," Veranis said. "So yes."

Varyn clapped a hand on Veranis's shoulder. "That means we get to annoy you across a continent."

"I've never regretted marriage more."

Niran grinned. "We're great travel companions. Aetherion only broods half the time. I only set fires occasionally. Varyn can be bribed with wine."

"Sounds like hell," Veranis muttered. But his voice was fond.

It caught Dorian off guard.

The way Veranis softened around them. The way the brothers didn't flinch at his presence. The way Aetherion actually relaxed.

This wasn't an act.

They trusted him.

They loved him.

And it made Dorian feel like the odd piece in someone else's puzzle.

The tension must've shown on his face, because Veranis looked at him again.

"I don't expect your trust," he said quietly. "Not yet."

Dorian didn't respond.

Couldn't.

Veranis gave a slight nod, then turned toward the path that led back toward the barracks.

"I'll be ready at dawn."

They watched him go.

Niran nudged Dorian after a moment. "He's a lot. I get it."

"He's not bad," Varyn added. "Just... hard to read."

Aetherion simply said, "He's family."

And that was the difference.

They'd chosen him.

Dorian hadn't.

Not yet.

But as the stars brightened over Aresia and the wind stirred across the cliffs, Dorian realized maybe—just maybe—he wasn't as far from belonging as he thought.

They were leaving for Aegyptia at first light.

And for the first time in a long time, he wasn't running alone.

Chapter Twelve

An Offer from the Shadows

"Even silence sings, if you know how to listen."—Teachings of the First Raevnir

☐

The desert of Aegyptia was nothing but scorching sun and endless dunes.

Dorian had never been this hot in his life.

His clothes—already falling apart thanks to his fantastic luck—were now sticking to his skin in ways that felt like a personal attack. His boots were filled with sand, his face was probably burning off, and now he was convinced the sun was personally trying to kill him.

"This is hell," he muttered.

Veranis, who somehow looked completely fine despite the unbearable heat, barely glanced at him. "You've never been to hell. This is just sand."

Dorian scowled. "Sand that's trying to kill me," he corrected.

The heat shimmered around them, waves of distortion rising from the dunes like something alive. They had been traveling for hours, the weight of the sun pressing down on them like a god's hand.

Aetherion led the way, as silent and unreadable as ever, while Varyn and Niran walked a few steps behind, bickering in their usual fashion.

"Do you want to make a bet, brother? Will it be Dorian that collapses first, or will you collapse first?" Varyn smirked, his silver wings flicking slightly.

"You wound me, brother—my flames do not break so easily." Niran shot back, his fiery wings twitching.

"Your fire is already ash, dear brother."

"Mir, you think too highly of yourself. I am fireborn!"

"Fireborn my ass," Aetherion muttered, already done with them.

Dorian was about to ask why they weren't dying in the heat like normal people, when—

The air shifted.

Not from the heat. From something else.

The world around them went still.

Dorian's skin prickled, a warning thrumming beneath his ribs.

Ahead of them, the dunes rippled, distorting like a mirage. Like reality itself was bending.

And then—

A shadow stepped forward.

Dorian knew who it was before he even spoke.

The way he moved—too smooth, too comfortable, like he belonged anywhere he decided to stand. The way the air shifted around him, bending to his will.

Loki looked exactly how Dorian imagined a trickster god would.

Relaxed. At ease. Like none of this was remotely his problem.

Which meant it absolutely was.

Varyn and Niran froze.

Dorian could see it—the flicker of confusion, the unspoken tension. Like their bodies knew something their minds didn't.

And then Loki smiled. Sharp. Too knowing.

"My sons," he said smoothly.

Silence.

Varyn's expression darkened instantly. His wings flared just slightly as he stepped in front of Niran, blocking him from Loki's view.

"You're not our father," he growled.

Niran, still half-shadowed behind him, added, "Yeah, our dad is dead."

Loki sighed. "Ah, so your mother never told you." His silver eyes gleamed with mock disappointment. "Pity."

Dorian had no idea what the fuck was happening, but he knew a dire situation when he saw one.

Varyn's hands curled into fists. "You're not our father."

Loki tilted his head. "A technicality. But one we should discuss."

The air around them felt thicker now, heavier.

Dorian barely had time to process before Loki's gaze flicked toward him.

"You don't have to run," Loki said smoothly. "You could have unimaginable power."

Dorian's jaw locked. He knew a lie when he heard one.

Veranis moved before Dorian could.

His silver wings unfolded slightly, subtly blocking Dorian from Loki's view.

"We're done here," Veranis said. Calm. Unshaken. Absolute.

Loki sighed. "You always were the boring one."

Before he could take another step—

A new voice cut through the air.

"And you need to learn to back off."

The desert wind ripped through the dunes as Velocia appeared—no, descended.

Her indigo-feathered wings snapped wide, the constellation-like patterns gleaming beneath the searing sunlight. Golden sand swirled around her, caught in the force of her arrival.

Her amber eyes burned.

And she was furious.

"Get away from my sons," she hissed, stepping between them like a living barrier. "You have no right to them. Not after what you put me through. And I will not have you corrupting them just for your own twisted games!"

Loki's smile didn't falter. But something in his gaze shifted.

Dorian saw it. A flicker of something ancient. Something cruel.

Velocia's wings flared wider, her fangs bared. The serrated edges caught the sunlight, glinting like polished ivory.

The air crackled.

Dorian's pulse pounded.

And then—

The ground shook.

A roar split the sky.

A massive, shadowed form descended from the clouds, blocking out the sun itself.

Kael.

His obsidian-black scales glinted like polished onyx, the copper tips of his wings burning like molten fire. His crystalline blue eyes locked onto Dorian, unblinking.

And beside him—

Aurora.

Her scales shimmered between emerald, cerulean, and violet, her wings flaring wide like ribbons of the northern lights.

Dorian couldn't move.

Kael's voice rumbled like thunder.

"Hand over the boy."

And just like that—

They were out of time.

Chapter Thirteen

Battle in Cairavia

"Let the gods count the dead. We only count the survivors."—Aegyptean War Hymns

The port city of Cairavia was chaos.

Flames climbed the skyline, smoke curling into the air like fingers of some ancient god reaching for the heavens. The scent of burning wood and seawater mixed with the metallic tang of blood.

Screams.

The clash of steel.

The ground shook as Kael descended, his obsidian wings blotting out the sun. The moment his talons met the sand, the earth cracked beneath him, the sheer weight of his form sending a tremor through the city.

And beside him—Aurora.

Where Kael was all shadow and fury, Aurora was the sky itself made flesh. Her scales shimmered between emerald, cerulean, and violet, her 130-foot wings unfurling in a cascade of light. Where she landed, the very air hummed with power.

Dorian felt his stomach drop.

They were not escaping this unscathed.

Aetherion was already moving, his sword gleaming silver as he sprinted forward, wings flaring wide. Varyn was right behind him, his blade curved like a predator's fang.

Kael turned to them, and smiled.

The battle began.

Kael didn't waste time with words.

His wings snapped once and he lunged.

Aetherion met him head-on, their blades clashing with a sound like thunder. The impact sent shockwaves through the sand, blasting debris into the air.

Varyn struck low, his movements fast, calculated, but Kael was too damn strong. His tail whipped around—Varyn barely dodged, rolling through the sand to avoid being impaled.

Kael laughed, deep and rumbling. "Is that all?"

Aetherion's eyes burned storm-blue.

"Not even close."

Lightning crackled across his blade, the air splitting with raw energy. He swung—Kael blocked with an armored forearm, but the force sent him skidding back, sand exploding beneath his feet.

Varyn moved in a blur, his sword slicing toward Kael's ribs. This time—Kael wasn't fast enough.

The blade cut deep.

Kael snarled, his tail whipping out violently. Varyn managed to dodge half a second too late—the strike clipped his side, sending him crashing through a market stall.

Aetherion didn't flinch.

He pressed the attack, his sword a blur of silver and storm light.

Kael roared, the ground shaking beneath his fury.

Veranis vs. Aurora

Aurora was faster than she looked.

One moment, she was still—the next, she was on Veranis.

He barely had time to move before her claws slashed through the air where his throat had been.

Veranis ducked, wings twisting, flipping backward just before she could tear into him. "Rushing me already?" He smirked, because of course he did. "Desperate, are we?"

Aurora snapped her fangs, missing him by inches.

Veranis moved like a ghost, his silver wings cutting through the smoke. His daggers flashed, slicing toward her exposed side—but she was ready.

Light exploded from her, a pulse of energy so blinding it turned the world white.

Veranis hit the ground hard, skidding across the sand.

Aurora landed gracefully, tilting her head. "You're arrogant."

Veranis pushed himself up, grinning despite the blood trickling down his temple. "And you're predictable."

His shadow moved.

Not like something following light—but like something alive.

And then—he vanished.

Aurora's eyes narrowed.

The battle was just beginning.

Dorian ran.

His lungs burned, his legs screamed, but stopping wasn't an option.

Behind him, the city was collapsing into war.

Kael's roars shook the streets. Aurora's light flared against the storm-clouded sky. Aetherion, Varyn, and Veranis were fighting like demons, but Dorian wasn't built for this.

Not yet.

Beside him, Niran was running too, his fire-colored wings tucked close. "We need to get to the docks!"

Dorian didn't argue.

They sprinted through the narrow streets, dodging flaming wreckage and broken stalls. The air was thick with magic, with death, with something else—

Something wrong.

Niran stumbled, his breath hitching. "Wait—"

Dorian skidded to a stop. "What?"

Niran's eyes had gone distant. His fingers clutched at his skull.

And then—he saw.

Not the city.

Not the battle.

Something else.

The vision hit like a hammer.

Flames.

Shadows.

A great beast rising from the abyss, its eyes endless, its hunger all-consuming.

A throne of bone. A sky split apart.

And Dorian—standing at the center of it all.

Niran's breath came in ragged bursts. He staggered back, his hands shaking.

"No," he whispered. "No, no, no—"

Dorian grabbed his arm. "What did you see?"

Niran's pupils were blown wide. He looked at Dorian like he was something else. Something terrible.

"You."

The world burned around them.

Chapter Fourteen

The Aftermath of Cairavia

"You cannot unmake a choice. You can only bury it."—Elysian Scholar

Dorian's ears were still ringing.

The battle had torn through Cairavia like a storm, leaving nothing but flames, rubble, and bodies in its wake.

The docks—their only chance of escape—were in ruins.

Ships burned, their masts collapsing in slow, agonizing groans. The water churned with wreckage and blood, the bodies of mercenaries, Syndicate killers, and soldiers alike floating among the debris.

Dorian forced himself to breathe. To move.

"Niran!"

Niran was still on his knees, his face pale, his wings trembling.

Dorian grabbed his arm, trying to shake him back to reality. "We have to go."

Niran's pupils were still too wide. Still seeing something else.

His breath hitched, his hands clenching into fists. "You don't understand."

Dorian scowled. "I really don't have time to."

Another explosion rocked the city, sending a fresh wave of fire into the sky.

Veranis landed beside them, wings folding, eyes sharp. "We need to move. Now."

Dorian yanked Niran to his feet, practically dragging him forward.

They had to get out of here.

Aetherion's sword was slick with blood.

Kael was still standing, but the battle had cost him. His scales were cracked, dark ichor dripping from a wound in his side where Varyn's blade had struck deep.

But he was still smiling.

"You're not bad," Kael admitted, rolling his shoulders, wings twitching slightly. "But you're still mortal."

Aetherion didn't answer. Didn't waste breath on words.

Varyn, though—Varyn was grinning.

"Then come find out how fragile we really are," he taunted.

Kael's eyes flashed.

He lunged.

Aetherion met him mid-air, sword colliding with claws, the force of impact splitting the sand beneath them.

Varyn moved in a blur, dodging Kael's tail by inches before slicing upward—but Kael was ready this time.

A massive blast of fire roared from his jaws.

Aetherion barely had time to throw up a shield of energy, the impact knocking both him and Varyn backward.

They were running out of time.

Aurora was still fighting Veranis in the skies above, but she wouldn't be distracted forever. And now—Kael wasn't playing anymore.

"We need to go," Aetherion muttered.

Varyn glanced toward the city. Toward where their family was.

And then—he nodded.

They moved.

Velocia's wings cut through the smoke, her amber eyes blazing with fury.

She had seen too much fire. Too much destruction. Too much death.

She had felt her sons in danger.

And now, she was done.

Loki was watching from a rooftop, lounging like this was all a game.

Because to him, it was.

"You're enjoying yourself," she snarled.

Loki's grin widened. "Of course I am."

Velocia moved.

One second, she was on the ground. The next, she had him pinned against a shattered wall, her claws pressing against his throat.

"You have no claim over my sons," she hissed.

Loki laughed softly. "Yet here we are."

Velocia's wings flared wider. "You have no idea how close you are to dying."

"Oh, I do," Loki said, entirely too calm.

Then he leaned in slightly. "But we both know you won't kill me. Not yet."

Velocia bared her fangs.

But he was right.

And that infuriated her more than anything.

Dorian could barely see through the smoke.

The docks were gone—completely destroyed.

Which meant they had one chance left.

"There's a side exit," Niran rasped. His voice was shaky, but his mind was clear now. "Through the old market."

Dorian didn't question it.

They ran.

But something was wrong.

The air felt thicker.

The world was shifting around him.

And then—the vision struck.

Fire.

The abyss.

The same great beast from Niran's vision, its endless eyes staring straight at him.

A voice, low and endless, whispered through his mind.

"You cannot run from what you are."

Dorian collapsed to his knees.

And for the first time—he felt it.

The Eye of Shadows wasn't lost.

It was inside him.

Chapter Fifteen

The Fracture

"A retreat is not weakness. It is the meaning of death."—Stormrheim Codex

Smoke clung to Dorian's skin like regret.

The city still burned behind them, and yet the world had gone quiet—too quiet. The kind of quiet that only comes after devastation has run its course and left nothing behind but ash.

They had made it out.

Barely.

The old market had opened into a winding trail that cut through the ruins along the city's edge—what used to be a smuggler's path, now just another broken road leading away from hell.

The group moved in silence. No one spoke. No one dared.

Dorian kept glancing at Niran.

The younger twin hadn't said a word since the vision. Since he'd looked at Dorian like he was some kind of monster.

And Dorian—Dorian didn't know what he'd seen either. Just that it hadn't been good.

Every time he blinked, he still felt the beast's eyes on him.

The Eye was inside him.

And something was waking.

He didn't want to talk about it.

He didn't want to think about it.

But he could feel the way the others watched him now. Like something about him had shifted—and they didn't know what it meant yet.

Hell, neither did he.

Velocia walked ahead, her wings tucked close, eyes scanning the horizon like she expected the sky to fall again. Veranis trailed her silently, shoulders stiff, his usual arrogance dulled beneath exhaustion. His knuckles were bloodied.

Aetherion didn't speak much, but he never left Dorian's side. Not out of comfort—out of caution. His hand hovered near his sword hilt every time Dorian stumbled or gasped or so much as twitched the wrong way.

And Dorian noticed.

Of course he did.

They reached the edge of a dune slope that overlooked the outskirts of Cairavia. The flames still licked at the horizon, a reminder of the gods and monsters that had torn it apart.

Varyn crouched near the ridge, scanning ahead.

"Trade routes are gone," he said, voice low. "We'll have to cut east and hope we hit the ridge pass before nightfall."

"No ships," Veranis muttered, arms crossed. "That's going to slow us."

Velocia didn't turn. "We don't have a choice."

"Isn't that the theme of this whole cursed adventure?" Dorian snapped before he could stop himself.

The words were sharper than he meant. Raw. Too loud in the cold silence.

Niran flinched.

Everyone stilled.

Dorian's breath came shallow. His hands curled into fists.

"I didn't ask for this," he muttered, voice lower now, but still tight. "I didn't ask to be dragged halfway across the world. To be hunted. To have this thing—" he pressed a trembling hand against his chest, "—inside me."

Niran stepped forward. His expression was unreadable. Too blank.

"You think you're the only one who didn't ask for any of this?"

Dorian met his eyes. "You're the one who looked at me like I was going to end the world."

Niran didn't deny it.

Didn't speak.

He just stared.

And that—more than words—set something inside Dorian on fire.

"You had a vision," Dorian hissed. "You saw something, didn't you?"

"I saw you," Niran said, quiet and brittle. "Burning everything. Standing in a sea of bones. And smiling."

The words hit like a punch.

And for a second—Dorian didn't breathe.

Velocia turned sharply, her eyes blazing. "That's enough."

But it wasn't.

Because Varyn stepped between them before Dorian could speak again.

"Stop," he said to Niran, his voice colder than usual. "You're not helping."

"I'm telling the truth."

"Doesn't mean it needs to be said."

Aetherion stood at Dorian's shoulder now. Silent. Steady.

Dorian wanted to scream.

Wanted to run.

But he didn't.

He just stood there, caught between silence and the weight of something he couldn't claw out of himself.

Velocia looked at them all—her sons. Her chaos. Her burdens.

And Dorian.

The outsider.

The cursed.

She exhaled slowly.

"We keep moving. When we reach Haventhorn, we rest. Until then—save your rage for the things that deserve it."

Niran didn't respond.

Varyn ran a hand down his face. "Well. That went well."

Veranis watched from a few paces back, his expression unreadable.

Dorian turned from them, unable to meet anyone's gaze.

Especially Aetherion's.

Especially Niran's.

He sat that night away from the others—curled near the embers of a dying fire, the cold creeping in.

He stared at his hands. At the place where the symbols burned under his skin.

He had no idea what he was becoming.

But whatever it was…

It was already starting to cost him.

Far away, in the deep places where gods whisper and shadows breathe, something ancient stirred.

And it remembered him.

Chapter Sixteen

The Road to Stormeheim

"The stars we chase are already within us."—

Teachings of the First Raevnir

The desert had nearly killed them.

The battle in Cairavia had left scars. Some physical. Some deeper.

And now—Stormrheim.

They traveled north, leaving the burning remains of Cairavia behind, crossing the last stretch of Aegyptia's dunes before reaching Haventhorn—the final trade city before the frozen wastes of Frostvyrd.

The air was already colder.

Dorian could feel the change in the wind, the shift in pressure, the way the sun seemed less oppressive. It should have been a relief after the hellish heat, but it wasn't.

Because something was wrong.

He hadn't had a vision since the docks. Hadn't felt the pull of the Eye of Shadows clawing at his mind. But that didn't mean it was gone.

It meant it was waiting.

The town of Haventhorn was small, built into the crags of the northern cliffs, the last true settlement before the tundra took over.

The streets were quieter than they should have been. Not empty, but cautious. People watched them pass—some curious, some wary.

Dorian had learned to recognize a city on edge.

Something had happened here.

Aetherion noticed it too. He glanced at Velocia, his storm-blue eyes sharp. "They're afraid."

Velocia nodded. "We should keep moving."

Veranis, naturally, looked unfazed. He adjusted his cloak and stretched, looking around like they weren't potentially walking into yet another mess. "Fear is natural when you live this close to the wastes. This city is a threshold. Step beyond it, and you're in Frostvyrd."

Dorian pulled his cloak tighter. "Fantastic. More freezing, near-death experiences. Just what I wanted."

Varyn smirked. "Oh, come now, street rat. Don't tell me you're cold already."

Niran laughed. "He'll be frozen solid before we even reach the border."

Dorian shot them both a murderous glare. "I hate both of you."

Veranis grinned. "That's the spirit."

Haventhorn's largest inn was barely more than a glorified outpost, built for travelers heading into the north.

It was there that Aetherion finally spoke.

They sat around the hearth, the fire crackling against the bitter cold creeping in from the north.

Dorian still felt off. The warmth didn't settle into him right.

Aetherion watched him, unreadable as always. Then, finally—

"The Eye is inside you."

Silence.

Dorian stilled. He hadn't said it out loud before. No one had.

But Aetherion knew.

Velocia's gaze was steady, but tense. Veranis leaned back in his chair, watching with mild interest but not interrupting.

It was Varyn who broke the silence. "That explains why everything wants to kill you."

Dorian shot him a look. "Wow. Thanks. So helpful."

Aetherion ignored them both. "The Eye of Shadows was never meant to be possessed by a mortal." His gaze was cold. Measured. "It's already changing you, isn't it?"

Dorian hesitated.

His first instinct was to lie. To say no. But the truth was already burning inside him.

Yes.

He felt the weight of it. The power. The hunger.

And worst of all—he didn't know if he could fight it.

Aetherion's voice was low. "You need to understand something. Power like that—it doesn't just give. It takes. It will hollow you out, wear you down until there's nothing left but the thing it wants you to be."

Dorian clenched his fists. "Then what the hell am I supposed to do?"

Aetherion exhaled slowly. "Survive long enough to figure that out."

They left Haventhorn at dawn.

The path into Frostvyrd was unforgiving. The moment they left the last of the cliffs behind, the temperature plummeted.

The winds howled, carrying flecks of ice that cut like knives. The sky was a dull, merciless gray.

Dorian had never been this cold in his life.

"Fucking hell," he muttered, wrapping his cloak tighter.

Niran grinned, fire flickering over his fingertips. "Want me to warm you up?"

Dorian didn't trust him not to set him on fire. "I'll pass."

Velocia walked ahead, her wings tucked tight, her eyes sharp as she scanned the tundra. She had been tense since last night.

Veranis walked beside her, more serious than usual. "You're worried."

Velocia didn't deny it. "Something feels wrong."

Aetherion nodded. "The air is too still."

Dorian was about to ask what the hell that meant—

When the ground trembled.

Varyn's head snapped up. "Tell me that was normal."

It wasn't.

The wind shifted.

And then—

From the ice, something rose.

Not a beast. Not a man.

Something worse.

And just like that, the hunt began again.

Chapter Seventeen

The Frozen Dead

"Glory is the most fragile armor of all."—Aegyptean War Hymns

The ground trembled.

Dorian's breath curled in the frigid air, his pulse hammering as the ice groaned beneath them.

Something was moving.

Not in the sky. Not in the distance. Beneath their feet.

The tundra lurched, snow splitting apart as something massive shifted beneath the surface.

Niran swore, his flames flickering to life, casting golden light against the white expanse.

"Tell me this is normal," Varyn muttered.

"It's not," Aetherion said flatly.

Then—the ice cracked.

Something burst upward from the frozen depths.

A claw. Rotting flesh stretched over jagged bone, dark sigils carved into decayed skin.

And then another.

And another.

Dorian barely had time to react before the dead dragged themselves free of the ice.

They weren't just corpses.

They were ancient. Twisted. Preserved in the ice for centuries.

Their armor was blackened with frost, their weapons worn but deadly. Their eyes—hollow, yet burning with an unnatural blue light.

Aetherion's grip tightened on his sword. "Frostborn."

Velocia cursed under her breath. "How many?"

Veranis grinned, because of course he did. "More than enough to keep us entertained."

The dead lurched forward.

And the battle began.

Dorian vs. the Undead

Dorian barely had time to draw his dagger before one of the Frostborn lunged.

He ducked, barely avoiding the jagged blade swinging toward his throat.

Then another one was on him.

Too fast. Too strong.

Cold fingers closed around his wrist, jerking him forward. His vision blurred—the glowing sigils carved into its bones flared, and for a second—

He saw something else.

The past.

The moment this thing had died.

A battlefield.

Ice and blood.

And a king, standing at the center of it all—wearing a crown of shadows.

Dorian gasped, wrenching free.

The vision shattered.

And the Frostborn came again.

Velocia moved like a hurricane.

Her wings unfurled, the constellation-like markings blazing against the frozen air.

She wasn't just fighting.

She was tearing through the undead like they were nothing.

One came at her from behind—she spun, claws flashing, her fangs bared. The creature didn't even have time to react before she ripped it apart, the force of her strike sending frozen bone scattering across the tundra.

Another lunged.

She let it get close.

Then, in one fluid motion—she snapped its neck.

Loki had called her a plaything, once.

But she had become a monster of her own making.

And she would never be caged again.

Aetherion fought with precision.

Every movement calculated, every strike measured. His blade cut through frozen sinew and shattered bone, lightning crackling along its edges.

Varyn was faster.

His sword sliced through the air, every movement fluid, effortless. He fought like he was dancing, weaving between enemies, striking where they were weakest.

But there were too many.

The Frostborn kept rising.

"We can't keep this up forever!" Varyn shouted, slicing through another.

Aetherion didn't look away from the fight. "We won't have to."

Because something was coming.

Something worse.

The wind shifted.

The undead froze.

For the first time—they hesitated.

The ice groaned again.

And then—the earth split open.

A figure emerged from the depths of the frozen wasteland.

Tall. Wrapped in ancient armor, lined with frost and shadow. A helm, cracked down the center, revealing empty eyes that burned with blue fire.

The Frost King.

He had waited centuries for this moment.

And now—his gaze fell upon Dorian.

"You carry the Eye," he rumbled.

Dorian's blood turned to ice.

Chapter Eighteen

The Tomb of the Eye

"To ask the right question is more dangerous than to give the wrong answer."— Elysian Scholar

The wasteland stretched before them—a graveyard of ice and ruin.

Eryndor.

Once, it had been a kingdom. Now, it was little more than shattered stone and whispers of the past.

Dorian pulled his cloak tighter around himself, his breath curling in the frigid air. The battle against the Frostborn had left them bruised and exhausted, but there was no time to recover.

Not when the Tomb of the Eye was waiting.

And not when something else was watching.

They walked through the remnants of war.

Weapons half-buried in the snow, bones frozen in place where warriors had fallen. Banners long torn apart by the wind; their sigils barely recognizable.

Niran ran a hand over one of the broken blades. "This was the last battle of Rhexion."

Velocia's eyes darkened. "I remember."

Dorian turned toward her. "You were here?"

Velocia didn't look at him. Didn't answer immediately. When she finally spoke, her voice was quiet.

"We all were."

And that was the end of it.

They kept moving.

The entrance was carved into the cliffs, a massive gate of blackened stone, untouched by time. Strange symbols etched into the rock pulsed faintly, reacting to their presence.

Dorian felt it.

The pull.

Like something inside was waiting for him.

Veranis let out a low whistle. "That looks… inviting."

Varyn smirked. "Shall we knock?"

Aetherion ignored them both, stepping forward. He pressed his palm against the stone. The symbols flared to life.

The gates rumbled open.

The air shifted.

Something stirred.

And then—the guardian stepped forward.

It was not alive.

Not in the way they were.

The guardian's body was woven from the very shadows of the tomb, its form shifting like mist given shape. Its eyes—empty, yet burning.

It spoke in a voice that did not echo, but simply existed, pressing against their minds like an ancient weight.

"To claim the Eye is to accept the cost."

Dorian felt the words inside his skull.

His breath hitched. "What cost?"

The guardian turned to him.

"The price of power is never freely given. It takes. It devours. It consumes."

Silence.

Velocia's fingers tensed against the hilt of her blade.

Dorian swallowed hard. "And if I don't take it?"

The guardian's voice was cold. "Then the world will burn."

Dorian could feel everyone watching him.

Waiting.

Aetherion's gaze was sharp. Measuring.

Velocia's was unreadable.

Niran looked worried.

And Veranis? Smirking, because of course he was.

But this wasn't a joke.

Dorian turned back to the guardian. "What if I fail?"

The guardian tilted its head.

"Then you will not live long enough to regret it."

The doors groaned open.

The path to the Eye was waiting.

And Dorian took the first step forward.

Chapter Nineteen

Weight of the Past

"Every wall was built on the bones of those who stood alone."—Stormrheim Codex

The wind howled through the bones of Eryndor.

They had stopped to rest beneath the jagged remains of an old war monument—half-buried in the snow, its surface cracked by time and fire. A statue once carved in honor of a hero now looked more like a frozen corpse reaching skyward.

Niran sat beneath it, knees drawn to his chest, staring at the sky.

He wasn't cold.

He didn't feel anything at all.

The others were scattered nearby—Velocia speaking quietly with Veranis, Dorian pacing along the edge of a cliff that overlooked the broken city below, Aetherion sharpening his blade with deliberate silence, and Varyn watching Niran like he expected him to shatter.

He wasn't wrong.

Niran's fingers flexed against the frozen stone.

He couldn't get the voice out of his head.

You've always known, haven't you? That you were different.

Loki's words, curling in his mind like smoke. Like poison.

Because the truth was—he had known.

Something inside him had always felt... off. Like there was too much chaos inside his skin, like he was always walking the line between fire and ruin. His magic burned hotter than it should. His emotions twisted too fast. His nightmares weren't just dreams—they were memories.

His mother tried to hide it. So did Aetherion.

But Niran had never been stupid.

He had just hoped—hoped—that if he ignored the wrongness, it would fade.

It hadn't.

And now Loki had spoken it aloud.

God blood.

His blood.

Niran felt sick.

"You gonna say something?" Varyn's voice cut through the silence, low but sharp. He crouched a few feet away, his usual smirk gone. "You've been spiraling since we left the tomb."

Niran didn't look at him. "You heard him."

"Yeah. I also heard Velocia threaten to rip out his spine." Varyn's eyes narrowed. "So, forgive me if I'm not immediately signing up to believe the world's most manipulative god."

"He wasn't lying," Niran said flatly.

"That doesn't make it true."

Silence stretched between them.

"I felt it," Niran whispered. "When he said I was his. It clicked. Like some part of me recognized him. And it shouldn't have."

Varyn sat down beside him. Close, but not touching.

"Do you remember when we were kids?" Varyn asked after a moment. "You used to set things on fire just by getting scared. One time you almost torched the temple in Virelos because you thought a bird was following you."

Niran gave a shaky breath. "It was following me."

"Right. My point is—you've always been a little unhinged. But you've always been you. That doesn't change just because some god decides to claim you like a trophy."

Niran's laugh was hollow. "Easy for you to say. You didn't feel what I felt."

Varyn looked at him then—really looked.

And Niran hated the pity in his eyes.

"You think I haven't felt it?" Varyn said quietly. "You think I don't wake up some nights and wonder if we're just ticking bombs in someone else's game?"

Niran finally turned to him. "Then why aren't you afraid?"

"I am. I'm just too stupid to show it."

Niran gave a weak, broken laugh.

Aetherion approached then, casting a long shadow across the snow.

His gaze flicked between the twins. "We move soon."

Niran nodded, but didn't rise.

Aetherion didn't leave. His voice lowered. "Loki will try again."

Niran's jaw clenched.

"I know."

"He sees you as a flaw in the design," Aetherion said. "Something unformed. Something he can mold."

"I'm not weak."

"No. But you're hurting."

That, somehow, felt worse.

Niran stood abruptly, brushing snow off his coat. "I'm fine."

"You're lying."

"I said I'm fine."

Aetherion didn't push. He just nodded once, stepped back into the falling snow.

Varyn stayed beside Niran.

"You don't have to go through this alone," he said, voice low. "I know it feels like the world is tilting under you. But I'm still here."

Niran didn't respond.

Because he wasn't sure if he wanted to be saved.

And in the distance, where the tomb loomed like a black wound against the ice—

Something was watching.

Waiting.

And inside Niran's chest, the god blood stirred.

Chapter Twenty

The Lies of Gods

"Fire is neither cruel nor kind. It only reveals."—Teachings of the First Raevnir

Dorian hadn't expected silence.

The inside of the Tomb of the Eye was vast, the ceiling lost to shadows, the walls lined with ancient carvings—stories of battles, of power, of the rise and fall of kings.

And at the center—a massive stone dais.

Waiting.

The Eye of Shadows wasn't here. Not yet.

But Dorian could feel it.

Like a pulse in the air. A whisper at the edges of his mind.

Waiting.

A slow clap echoed through the tomb.

Dorian tensed.

He didn't need to turn around to know who it was.

"Loki," Velocia hissed, stepping forward, wings flaring wide.

Loki smirked, stepping out of the shadows, his form too casual, too effortless, like none of this was his problem.

But his eyes—too sharp. Too knowing.

"Mother," he greeted smoothly, looking toward Velocia with an expression that could only be described as mocking affection. Then, his gaze slid to Varyn and Niran.

"And my sons."

Varyn's hand immediately went to his sword. "You're not our father."

Loki tilted his head. "A technicality, really. But the blood in your veins says otherwise."

Niran was silent.

Watching.

"Lies," Varyn snapped.

Loki sighed dramatically. "Ah, you wound me, truly." He took a step forward. "But I'm afraid this is not a lie. You are not just warriors. Not just mortals. You are divine. Born from chaos itself. You are my blood."

Silence.

Aetherion stepped forward, blocking them from Loki's reach. "You think we don't already know what you are?"

Loki's smirk widened. "Of course, you do. But they didn't." He nodded toward Varyn and Niran.

Dorian glanced between them.

Varyn's expression was cold, calculating. He wasn't buying it.

But Niran…

His fingers twitched.

Loki saw it. Latched onto it.

"You've always known, haven't you?" Loki murmured, looking directly at Niran. "Felt different. Felt stronger. Felt like there was something more inside of you."

Niran swallowed.

"You don't have to be his lapdogs," Loki said smoothly, nodding toward Aetherion. "He's been lying to you this whole time."

Varyn laughed coldly. "Right. And we should trust you?"

Loki shrugged. "I have no reason to lie. I've already won."

That made Dorian's blood run cold.

Velocia's teeth bared. "You've won nothing."

Loki didn't even acknowledge her. His focus remained on Niran.

"You could be more. You could be great. And you don't even know it yet."

Niran's fingers curled into fists.

Aetherion spoke then. "Loki only takes. You know that."

But something had already shifted.

Varyn wasn't falling for it. But Niran?

Dorian saw it.

Saw the doubt.

The hesitation.

And that—that was exactly what Loki wanted.

The ground shook.

The air turned frigid.

A shadow fell over them as Kael descended into the tomb, his obsidian-black scales glinting in the torchlight.

Cryos followed, his massive ice-covered wings sending a gust of frozen wind through the chamber.

Kael's cold blue eyes locked onto Dorian.

"Step aside."

Veranis grinned. "You know, you could just ask nicely."

Kael's wings flared. "This is not a request."

Cryos stepped forward, voice like grinding ice. "The Eye does not belong to you. It belongs to dragonkind."

Dorian's pulse pounded.

This was not the time to be dealing with both Loki's manipulations and two ancient dragons.

But apparently, fate didn't give a shit about what he wanted.

Varyn grabbed Niran's arm. "Don't listen to him."

Niran yanked free. "You don't get it."

Dorian stepped in. "Niran, you know what Loki is. You know what he does. He manipulates; he twists things to make them work in his favor."

Niran's jaw tensed. But still, he hesitated.

Loki smiled. "Or maybe he finally sees the truth."

Velocia moved then. Her wings flared, eyes burning. "Get away from my son."

The moment tensed.

Aetherion gripped his sword.

Kael and Cryos watched with interest.

And then—the tomb began to collapse.

Chapter Twenty-One

The Visions of the Eye

"A king without war is a sword without land."—Aegyptean War Hymns

The world was falling apart.

The tomb trembled, dust and stone breaking loose from the high ceiling. The echoes of Kael's fury, Loki's manipulation, and Niran's doubt still rang in Dorian's head.

But none of it mattered.

Not anymore.

Not when the Eye was waiting.

Dorian barely registered the others shouting. Barely noticed the chaos unraveling around him.

Because the moment his fingers brushed the surface of the Eye—

Everything ceased to exist.

Dorian wasn't in the tomb anymore.

The world had shifted.

The sky was red. The ground cracked beneath his feet, molten fire bleeding from the earth like an open wound.

Cities lay in ruins. Armies—human, dragon, god-born—scattered in pieces.

And at the center of it all—

Himself.

But not the version he knew.

This Dorian stood on a throne of bone and shadow. His armor was blackened steel, lined with veins of crimson light. His eyes—empty, yet burning.

And the world bowed before him.

He saw Aetherion falling, sword shattered.

Velocia, wings broken, kneeling in chains.

Niran and Varyn standing at his side—one willingly, the other bleeding from the choice.

Veranis laughing in the dark, amused but untouched.

And at his feet, the world burning.

"This is what you could be."

A voice, deep and endless, slithered into his skull.

Dorian turned—and saw the true source of it all.

A shape in the abyss. Massive. Monstrous. Ancient.

The Shadow Dragon was watching.

The world shattered again.

A new vision rose from the ashes of the last.

This time, the sky was golden, streaked with silver light. The air was clean, unbroken by the scent of fire and death.

And there he was—but different.

This version of himself wore no armor, only a simple cloak, lined with silver embroidery. His eyes weren't empty voids, but storm-gray, sharp and clear.

And instead of ruling—he was leading.

Aetherion stood at his side, unbroken.

Velocia laughed, wings unbound, free.

Varyn and Niran were there—not as soldiers, but as brothers.

And the world—was whole.

The voice whispered again.

"This is what you could save."

The weight of the choice settled deep into his bones.

The power of the Eye could make one of these futures real.

But which one?

Which version of himself would he become?

The Stirring of Shadow

Dorian felt it before he heard it.

A shift. A tremor.

And then—

The void itself breathed.

The Shadow Dragon moved.

Not fully awake. Not yet.

But watching.

Waiting.

And hungry.

Dorian jerked back, gasping. The visions snapped apart like shattered glass.

He was on his knees, panting, the Eye pulsing beneath his fingers.

The tomb was still collapsing around him.

And somewhere, deep below them—

Shadow stirred.

Chapter Twenty-Two

The Cost of Power

"Madness and wisdom drink from the same well."—Elysian Scholar

Dorian was still gasping for breath, the visions tearing through his mind like jagged glass. The future he had seen—the destruction, the power, the choice—still burned behind his eyes.

But before he could even process it, before he could pull himself fully back into reality—

Niran moved.

"I can do it."

Dorian froze.

Slowly, he turned—just in time to see Niran stepping toward the Eye.

His hands were clenched into fists, his body taut with unspoken tension. And his eyes—his normally bright, flame-lit eyes—were locked onto the Eye of Shadows with something dangerously close to desperation.

Dorian's stomach dropped.

"Niran," Velocia warned, her wings flaring slightly. "Step away from it."

Niran didn't.

"You saw what it can do," he said, his voice sharp, edged with something unsteady. "I can control it."

"Are you insane?" Varyn snapped, stepping between him and the dais. "You just saw what it did to Dorian!"

"Yeah," Niran shot back, "and he's still standing."

Dorian opened his mouth, but Niran wasn't looking at him.

He was looking at Loki.

And Loki was smiling.

Oh, shit.

"Niran," Dorian said carefully, stepping forward. "This thing isn't meant to be controlled."

Niran didn't even blink. "I was born from chaos itself," he said, voice calm, but deadly. "If anyone can control it, it's me."

And before anyone could stop him—

Niran grabbed the Eye.

For a second, nothing happened.

Then—

Everything collapsed.

Niran screamed.

Not just in pain—in something deeper, something raw and unmaking.

The tomb trembled. The symbols carved into the walls flared violently to life, flickering between blinding gold and endless void. The air went thick and wrong, pressing in on Dorian's skin like invisible claws.

And Niran—

His body seized. His wings flared violently, shifting colors in rapid succession—red, orange, gold, black, white, silver—like the Eye was trying to decide what he was.

And failing.

Horribly.

Dorian lunged.

"Let it go!"

But Niran couldn't.

His hands were fused to the Eye, the black veins of its power crawling up his arms like living tendrils. His eyes rolled back, his mouth opening in a soundless scream.

Loki watched with mild interest. "Ah. There it is."

Dorian whipped toward him. "Do something!"

Loki tilted his head. "Why would I do that?"

Dorian swung.

His first collided with Loki's jaw, sending the trickster god staggering back. The grin never fully faded, but it wavered for just a second.

And then—

The ground split apart.

The tomb collapsed inward.

A wave of black fire erupted from the Eye, consuming everything.

Velocia grabbed Varyn, yanking him backward as the explosion hit. Veranis moved just as fast, pulling Dorian away before the force of the blast could rip him apart.

And at the center of it all—

Niran.

Still standing.

Still screaming.

The power of the Eye tore through him, and the more he tried to control it, the more it fought back.

And beneath them—deep below the tomb—

Something answered.

Grooms   Eye of Shadows

A single, massive pulse—like a heartbeat made

of fire and oblivion—shook the earth.

And for the first time in centuries,

Shadow woke up.

Chapter Twenty-Three

The Choice of the Eye

"The only clean blade is one never drawn."—

Stormrheim Codex

The tomb was gone.

Or at least—it was no longer stable.

Cracks splintered through the stone, the walls caving inward as Shadow's resurgence sent violent tremors ripping through the ruins.

Dorian barely had time to brace himself before a section of the ceiling crashed down, sending stone and debris scattering.

Somewhere through the dust, he heard Kael's roar—except this time, it wasn't a battle cry.

It was pain.

Dorian whipped around just in time to see Kael stagger.

The once-imposing dragon stumbled backward, his massive wings struggling to keep him upright. His obsidian-black scales—normally impenetrable—were split, jagged wounds carved through his body, dark ichor seeping into the dust.

Cryos lunged to catch him, but Kael was already falling.

Dorian's stomach twisted violently.

Kael—the dragon who had always been untouchable, always powerful—was dying.

And Shadow had barely begun to stir.

Velocia was the first to react. She rushed toward Kael, her wings flaring wide, anger and desperation warring in her expression.

But there was nothing she could do.

Kael collapsed.

And the earth shuddered beneath the weight of his body.

Dorian's pulse pounded.

This was it.

The prophecy was happening right in front of him.

Kael—the strongest of them all—had fallen. Shadow was waking.

And the Eye—still pulsing, still waiting, still demanding a choice—sat just beyond his reach.

Everything he had seen in the visions.

Everything he had feared.

This was the moment.

Dorian swallowed hard, his breath sharp and uneven. "Shit."

Varyn was still holding Niran upright, the younger twin barely conscious after the Eye had nearly consumed him. Veranis stood a few feet away, his normally amused expression void of humor.

Aetherion met Dorian's gaze.

He knew.

And so did Dorian.

There was no more running.

The world had narrowed down to one decision.

Dorian could walk away.

Let the Eye disappear. Let Shadow rise unchecked. Let fate tear itself apart.

Or—

He could claim it.

Risk everything.

Dorian's hands were shaking. He wasn't sure if it was fear, or the weight of something far bigger than himself settling into his bones.

He stepped forward.

His fingers closed around the Eye.

And time—

Stopped.

Chapter Twenty-Four

The Shattered Sky

"Balance is not peace. It is tension held sacred."—Teachings of the First Raevnir

The light above the tomb was wrong.

Too still. Too quiet. Too bright.

The sky hadn't broken yet—but it was about to.

They stood just outside the crumbling remains of the tomb, silence hanging over them like a blade.

Kael's body still smoldered where it had fallen. A crater carved from his collapse stretched across the mountainside. The heat of his dying breath still shimmered in the air, steam curling where it met the snow.

No one spoke.

Even Varyn—usually the first to crack a joke or spit some snide remark—stood stiff and silent, his gaze locked on the horizon like he expected the world to end any second.

And maybe it already had.

Dorian sat on a fractured stone slab, the Eye was still pulsing faintly in his hand. He hadn't let go. He wasn't sure he could.

The others hadn't gotten close since.

He felt… fractured. Not broken. Not yet. But the weight of the Eye was heavy in a way that couldn't be seen. A pressure behind his eyes. A tremor beneath his skin. Like his blood had started whispering secrets he wasn't meant to hear.

He wasn't sure if he was still entirely Dorian.

"Kael didn't deserve that," Niran muttered, his voice low, sharp. "Not like that."

"No one deserves to die like that," Velocia said softly.

She stood with her wings partially unfurled, the wind catching the stars across her feathers. She looked celestial. Eternal. But her eyes told a different story—tired, and furious, and mourning.

Her gaze drifted to her sons.

Aetherion. Varyn. Niran.

Still alive. Still whole.

But barely.

They were all changing, and she could see it happening in real time.

Dorian noticed it too.

The three brothers stood slightly apart now—still close, but… guarded.

Aetherion's silence had deepened. Varyn had grown sharper, more cynical. And Niran—Niran had a shadow behind his eyes now. Not just from the Eye's near-possession of him. From Loki's words. From the doubt he couldn't shake.

They were fraying.

And Dorian felt like he was the splinter that had driven itself between them.

"I saw the sky crack," he said suddenly. "When I took it. Just for a second. I felt something beyond it, like… like there was something alive up there, watching."

"Shadow is watching," Aetherion replied. "And not just watching. Awakening."

"Good," Veranis said from where he leaned against a shattered column. "I was starting to think this journey lacked dramatic flair."

Velocia shot him a look.

Veranis smiled, but it didn't reach his eyes.

No one else responded.

Because they all felt it now. In the air. In the wind. In their bones.

The sky was wrong.

The pressure built with every heartbeat. The wind carried whispers that weren't in any language they knew. The clouds had begun to form strange shapes, twisting spirals that mirrored the runes carved into the tomb.

And far in the distance—a line of black splitting the heavens.

It hadn't reached them yet.

But it would.

"We need to move," Velocia said. "We don't know what happens when the sky breaks. But it will break."

"Where do we go?" Dorian asked, his voice rough. "Now that I've taken this? Now that we've lost Kael?"

Aetherion stepped forward. "North."

"North?" Varyn asked, incredulous. "Into the glacier fields?"

"There's a temple buried beneath them. One that predates even Olympus. We'll find answers there. Or at least a chance to survive what's coming."

Niran scoffed. "You sound so confident."

"I'm not," Aetherion said. "But it's the only path left."

Veranis straightened. "Then let's not wait for the world to fall apart on top of us."

Still, none of them moved.

The sky cracked a little more.

Just a thin sliver. A fracture in reality.

Light poured through it—not sunlight. Not divine glow.

Something older.

And Velocia finally said what none of them wanted to admit.

"If Kael could fall," she whispered, "then we're not ready for what's coming."

Her sons looked at her.

Not as the immortal goddess of creation.

But as their mother.

She looked tired. For the first time, she looked afraid.

And Dorian understood.

This wasn't just a war between gods and mortals.

It was the kind of war that rewrote the bones of the world.

The Eye burned faintly in his hand.

He held it tighter.

And then—he stood.

"We'll face it," he said. "All of it."

Velocia met his gaze.

And nodded.

As the first crack of thunder ripped across the sky.

As if the heavens themselves were splitting open.

Chapter Twenty-Five

The War Begins

"Even the strongest oath wilts in the heat of the last breath."—Aegyptean War Hymns

Time stood still.

For a moment, there was only silence.

Then—the world shattered.

A pulse of energy ripped through the ruins, so vast and ancient that it wasn't just felt—it was imprinted into the very fabric of existence. The air tore apart like something vast and immeasurable had just exhaled for the first time in centuries.

And beneath them—deep in the abyss where Shadow had slumbered—

The dragon opened its eyes.

A single, monstrous breath rumbled through the tomb.

Not just sound—power.

The walls collapsed inward.

Dorian barely had time to react before the ground beneath him cracked wide open.

The Eye burned in his grasp, reacting to the shift, feeding off the chaos.

And far beyond the tomb—across all of Eldoria—

The world felt it.

From the emerald forests of Elysia to the storm-ridden cliffs of Stormrheim, from the scorched dunes of Aegyptia to the floating citadels of Valoria—

Everyone felt the change.

In the sky, thunder cracked without warning.

The seas pulled back before surging forward again, their tides no longer obeying the moons.

Flames erupted where no fire had been.

The winds turned violent.

Something was waking.

And the gods felt it first.

In the halls of Olympus—

Zeus stood at the peak of his throne room, lightning crackling in his palms. The other gods gathered in silence; their faces grim.

Ares grinned like war had come early. Athena sharpened her blade. Hades watched from the shadows; his expression unreadable.

And Hera—Hera whispered something under her breath, a prayer or a curse, no one could tell.

The war they had feared was here.

And then—

A single word echoed through the heavens, sent from a voice older than the gods themselves.

Shadow has returned.

Across the realms, the gods of Yggdrasil stirred.

Odin rose from his seat upon the Allfather's throne, ravens shrieking into the sky. Thor gripped Mjolnir tighter, his knuckles white.

Loki, standing in the shadows, only smiled.

Velocia had felt the shift before anyone else.

Even before the gods, even before the dragons, she had known.

Because the moment Dorian had taken the Eye, the moment Shadow had drawn its first breath—everything changed.

The final conflict had begun.

And she would not let her children face it alone.

She turned to Aetherion, Varyn, and Niran.

"Prepare yourselves," she said, her voice steady but heavy with something inevitable.

"War is here."

Epilogue

The Shadows Rise

"In the end, all roads return to silence."—Teachings of the First Raevnir

The sky was quiet.

Too quiet.

Velocia stood at the edge of Verdant Haven, her wings tucked tight against her back, her sharp amber gaze fixed on the stars.

They were shifting. Not in movement—but in meaning.

She had seen this once before.

Before the war of the gods. Before the great betrayals.

Before everything fell apart.

And now—it was happening again.

The constellations whispered of war.

Velocia exhaled slowly, closing her eyes for a brief moment.

She had known this was coming.

But knowing didn't make it any easier.

Behind her, Aetherion approached. His voice was steady, but there was an edge to it.

"It has begun."

Velocia nodded.

"And there is no stopping it now."

Far beneath the ruins, in a place where no light had touched in centuries,

Shadow spoke.

Its voice was not words, but a presence. A force.

The cavern walls quivered as the ancient beast stirred, its breath sending tremors through the dark.

The Eye was no longer sealed.

The world had shifted.

And so, the Shadow Dragon whispered to the void.

"The end has begun."

The words did not fade.

They echoed.

In a chamber of ever-shifting darkness, Loki leaned against a pillar, watching the chaos unfold like it was a story he had written long ago.

Because in a way—it was.

Everything was falling into place.

Kael was dying.

Shadow was waking.

The gods were preparing for war.

And Dorian—Dorian was no longer just a boy scraping by in Mythralis.

Loki smirked to himself, tipping his head slightly.

"Well," he murmured. "This is getting interesting."

Dorian sat in the ruins of the tomb, his body aching, his mind burning.

The Eye of Shadows was in his hand.

It wasn't pulsing. It wasn't glowing.

It was waiting.

For him.

For his choice.

And for the first time, he wasn't sure if he had taken it… or if it had taken him.

His fingers tightened around it.

The shadows curled at the edges of his vision.

And deep in his chest—he knew.

Nothing would ever be the same again.

What Remains

A Bonus Short Story

The light in the ruined chapel was gray.

Dorian sat with his back against a pillar, the stone cold through what was left of his shirt. Dust clung to his skin, dried blood stiff in the creases of his knuckles. The Eye of Shadows rested in the dirt beside him, inert. He hadn't touched it in hours. Or maybe days. Time had stretched, slow and senseless, into something that no longer felt real.

The roof was gone. Through the open sky, a single cloud drifted overhead—serene, unaware. Unbothered by the brokenness below. It didn't care that Kael was gone. That the seal was broken. That the boy who had once scraped by in Mythralis was now sitting in the ashes of something far larger than himself.

Footsteps stirred the silence.

Dorian didn't move.

Varyn stepped into the ruins without a sound, wings tucked close. His pale silver feathers shimmered faintly in the overcast light, shifting with an emotion he didn't voice. The wind caught in them as he slowed, folding them tight again. His soft charcoal gray hair was tousled, a smear of dried blood marking the line of his jaw. A shallow cut sat just above one brow, already healing.

He knelt a few feet away, unwrapping a small cloth bundle. Bread, dried fruit, water. Nothing warm. Nothing personal. Just something to break the silence if needed.

Dorian didn't touch it.

"You shouldn't be here," he said, voice low.

Varyn's amber eyes—fossilized gold and fire—studied him. "And yet here I am."

His wings shifted slightly, loosening, then settling again.

"You don't have to say anything," he added. "I'm not here to fix you."

Dorian exhaled, eyes still on the ground. "Then what are you here for?"

Varyn looked toward the Eye. His wings flicked once, subtle, almost imperceptible. "To remind you that you're not alone."

"I don't want reminders."

"Then don't take it as one."

The silence returned, pressing in from all sides. Distantly, a bird called. The wind pushed through the broken archways, carrying the scent of ash and stone.

Varyn settled in, legs folded beneath him. His wings adjusted behind him, slightly looser now. They moved when he did—not just as limbs, but like thoughts taking shape.

Dorian let his head tip back against the pillar. He stared at the sky. "I see him. Every time I blink. I see Kael falling. And I see myself—just… watching."

"You weren't just watching."

"You don't know that."

"I do."

Dorian dragged a hand down his face. He didn't have it in him to argue, not really.

"I didn't save him," he muttered. "All that power and I still couldn't stop it."

Varyn's wings stilled. His eyes lowered, just a little. "I know what that feels like."

Dorian glanced at him. "When?"

"There was a cave-in, near Mirath Ridge. Niran was trapped. I had the power. I had every advantage. And I couldn't get to him fast enough." He paused, voice quiet. "I pulled him out, eventually. But not before the rocks shattered half his leg. Not before he screamed."

Dorian didn't say anything.

"I saved him," Varyn continued. "But I still felt like I'd failed. Because I didn't save him perfectly. Because the pain got to him first."

The words sat between them like a stone too heavy to lift.

"I think," he said, softer, "when you care that much, it doesn't matter what you did. It matters what you couldn't undo."

Dorian's fingers twitched beside the Eye. He didn't touch it. He couldn't.

Varyn's wings flexed slightly, a faint lift and fall. Almost like he was grounding himself.

"I don't know who I am anymore."

"You're still you. Just more of you than before."

Dorian laughed, short and bitter. "That's a terrible thing to say."

"Maybe." Varyn looked up at the sky. "But it's still true."

They sat like that for a while. The light shifted.

"I used to tell Niran stories," Varyn said, not looking at him. "When the visions were bad. When the fear wouldn't go. I'd sit at the edge of his bed and talk until he fell asleep. It never fixed it. But it helped."

"Why are you telling me that?"

"Because you're sitting here like no one ever told you a story that mattered."

Dorian looked over at him. Varyn's wings had relaxed, feathers fluffed slightly in the wind.

"You don't need to be okay," Varyn said. "But you don't need to bleed alone either."

The quiet stretched, but it no longer felt empty.

Dorian didn't respond right away.

His gaze drifted toward the horizon, past the fractured stone and scattered debris. There was no sadness in his expression. Just weight.

"Kael was supposed to be invincible," he said, almost like he was speaking to himself. "Not just strong. Not just fast. But inevitable."

Varyn tilted his head, watching him. His wings flexed subtly—like something in Dorian's words had struck a chord.

"I spent my whole life hearing stories about dragons," Dorian went on. "How they shaped the world. How nothing could kill them. How their flames carved mountains, how the gods feared them. Kael believed every word of it. Believed he was untouchable. Like the world owed him something just for breathing."

He let out a quiet breath, not quite a laugh. "And still, he fell."

Varyn's wings lowered slightly, feathers catching the breeze.

"It doesn't make sense," Dorian said. "It's not grief. It's not guilt. It's just… disbelief."

He picked up a piece of broken stone and turned it over in his hand. "If a dragon can die, what else have we been wrong about?"

The weight of that hung between them.

Varyn didn't offer comfort. He didn't correct the thought.

Because he knew Dorian wasn't really asking.

He was unraveling.

Dorian didn't say anything. But he didn't look away.

The Eye stayed still in the dirt. Waiting. Always waiting.

But for now, Dorian wasn't.

Guide to Eldoria

Velocia: The Raevniran goddess of creation and protection. The mother of Aetherion, Varyn, and Niran. Mate to Veranis

Loki: The Stormrheim god of mischief and chaos. Biological father of Varyn and Niran

Odin: The Stormrheim god of wisdom and war. Known as the All-Father and leader of Yggdrasil

Zeus: King of the Elysian gods. God of the sky. Biological father of Aetherion

Ares: The Elysian god of war

Heracles: The Elysian god of agony

Athena: The Elysian goddess of Wisdom

Hera: The Elysian goddess of marriage and family

Veranis: The Warden of Shadow. Stepfather of Aetherion, Varyn, and Niran. Mate to Velocia

Varyn: The Quiet Menace. Older twin of Niran. Son of Velocia and Loki

Niran: The Fiery Flame. Younger twin of Varyn. Youngest of Velocia's sons. Son of Velocia and Loki

Aetherion: The Storm-Born. Oldest of Velocia's sons. Son of Velocia and Zeus

Dorian: A human who is spiritually connected to the Eye of Shadows. Street rat

Shadow: A dragon who created the Eye of Shadows. His history and birth is shrouded in mystery

Kael: The dragon general. The Black Flame

Aurora: A beautiful she-dragon. The Sky's Queen

Cryos: The Frost's Fury. An Arctic dragon

Frostborn: Frozen undead Stormrheim warriors that died violent deaths and were rejected by the gods

Raevnir: A species of dragon that live in human form. Key characteristics are large feathered wings and fangs. Key members are Velocia, Veranis, Aetherion, Varyn, and Niran

Eye of Shadows: An artifact that is said to be able to rewrite fate itself. Created by the dragon Shadow

Black Sun Syndicate: A group of mercenaries, pirates, and spies. They rule the shadowy underbelly of Eldoria

Mythralis: The central trading hub of Eldoria. Neutral ground and often left out of war

Stormrheim: The frozen north. Ruled by the Stormrheim gods. Key locations are Valkyngard, Haventhorn, Frosyvyrd, and Yggdrasil. Home to the lost city of Eryndor

Aegyptia: The hot desert to the east of Mythralis. Ruled by the Aegyptean gods. Key locations are Cairavia, Seraphis, Solaris, Pyramids of the Solaris Plateau, and the Valley of the Pharaohs

Elysia: The land to the south of Mythralis. Ruled by the Elysian gods. Key locations are Seaphos, Celestara, Sylvaria, Aresia, and Mount Olympus

Valoria: The land to the southwest of Mythralis. Ruled by King Haldor IV. Key location is Falconridge

Verdant Haven: The land to the west of Mythralis. Home of the dragons and the Raevnir. Created by Velocia, it is a haven to those who wish to avoid war or are seeking political asylum

Made in the USA
Coppell, TX
20 July 2025